SOUNDS

Dwayne Alexander Smith is the author of *Forty Acres*, which is in development at Netflix, with Jay-Z attached to produce. Pamela Samuels Young has been widely published across genres and Netflix is also developing her work, having optioned the first two books in her Vernetta Henderson series. Both authors received NAACP Image Awards, for *Forty Acres* and *Anybody's Daughter* respectively.

SOUNDS LIKE TROUBLE

A NOVEL

Pamela Samuels Young &
Dwayne Alexander Smith

faber

First published in the UK in 2026
by Faber & Faber Ltd
The Bindery
51 Hatton Garden, London
EC1N 8HN

First published in the USA in 2025
by Atria Books
an Imprint of Simon & Schuster, LLC

This book is a work of fiction. Any references to historical events, real people, or real places are used fictitiously. Other names, characters, places, and events are products of the author's imagination, and any resemblance to actual events or places or persons, living or dead, is entirely coincidental.

A CIP record for this book
is available from the British Library

ISBN 978–0–571–39364–0

Printed and bound in the UK on FSC® certified paper in line with our continuing
commitment to ethical business practices, sustainability and the environment.
For further information see faber.co.uk/environmental-policy

Our authorised representative in the EU for product safety is
Easy Access System Europe, Mustamäe tee 50, 10621 Tallinn, Estonia
gpsr.requests@easproject.com

1 3 5 7 9 10 8 6 4 2

For Cynthia Hebron,
my USC homegirl and biggest fan.
Thanks for always being there.

For my childhood friends from Crotona Park East in the Bronx—
where trouble found us daily, but friendship always had our backs.
We grew up fast, laughed hard, and learned even harder lessons.
Here's to a bond that time and distance will never break.

SOUNDS LIKE TROUBLE

Chapter 1

JACKSON

Despite the pair of armed thugs looming over me, it was a beautiful morning on Venice Beach.

I was seated on the patio of a hip beachfront coffee shop called Drip Drop. The tiny café was part of the carnival-like collage of souvenir shops, fast-food joints, weed dispensaries, psychic parlors, and artist stalls that lined the Venice boardwalk. My loft was just a block away, so on those mornings when I felt like giving my Keurig a rest, I'd throw on some sweatpants and wander down for a freshly brewed cup of vanilla-nut roast.

Prior to the arrival of my two surly visitors, I was sipping my coffee, watching the daily parade of local oddballs on the boardwalk, and strategizing about how to convince my new business partner, Mackenzie Cunningham, to double the furniture budget for our new office.

A little over a week ago, Mac and I received the keys. The 650-square-foot storefront space, located in downtown Culver City, was move-in ready. Unfortunately, Mac and I weren't ready to move in. The only things occupying our new place were a couple of cheap folding chairs and stacks of file-storage boxes. We couldn't agree on how to decorate the place. Mackenzie was all about function. A clean and professional look was good enough. I disagreed completely. Looking successful is just as, if not more, important than looking professional. When clients crossed our threshold, I wanted them to believe we were killing it. That we didn't need their business. That they'd be lucky to hire *us*. For weeks now we had visited dozens of furniture stores in search of a happy medium with zero success.

I was determined to have it out with Mac. Somehow convince her to see things my way. At least, that was my plan for today until my two visitors dropped into the Drip Drop.

"Sorry to bother you. Are you Jackson Jones?"

Admittedly, that opener threw me. When I first spotted the two African American men approaching me in designer suits with hip-level gun bulges, I instantly pegged them as professional law-breakers . . . AKA gangsters. Detectives can't afford Tom Ford and Hugo Boss. What I didn't expect was polite gangsters. Either way, I knew these brothers were trouble, so I went for a Hail Mary.

"Nope," I said, shaking my head and focusing on my coffee. "Sorry."

The two men didn't budge or take their eyes off me.

I figured the dude who spoke first was the one in charge. He had a perfectly cropped beard and better shoes than his pal, and I was pretty sure his nails were manicured. And although he was the younger of the two—I guessed early thirties—there was an aloof certainty in his eyes, like someone who thought he was untouchable.

"Mr. Jones," he said, "let's forgo the games." His voice was even-toned and measured, with an educated ring. He sounded more like a lawyer than a criminal. "My name is Prentice Willis. My father is Cedric Willis. I'm here on his behalf regarding an urgent matter."

I was mid-sip when Prentice brandished his father's name, and I damn near did a spit take. Cedric Willis was infamous. Known on the streets as Big Ced, head of the most powerful criminal organization in LA. Big Ced's crew didn't really have a name, but whispers called them the Black Mafia. Even the old-school Italian mob, which had slipped a rung or two over the decades, didn't screw with Big Ced's operation. His big black fist had a grip on everything, from traditional rackets like drugs, gambling, and sex trafficking to cutting-edge misdeeds like cyber scams and ransomware attacks. Over the last decade or so, Cedric Willis had launched many legit businesses in an effort to go corporate and rehabilitate his image, but everyone knew that Willis Worldwide was just a facade for a sophisticated and dangerous criminal empire.

I couldn't imagine what *urgent matter* had caused Big Ced to seek me out, but the very idea put a knot in my gut. Trying very hard to maintain my cool, I said to Prentice, "I don't believe I've ever met your father."

"You haven't. Not yet. That's why I'm here. He'd like a meeting at his office."

"About what?"

"All I'm allowed to say is what I've already said . . . it's an urgent matter."

"Oh, I see. He's looking to hire a private investigator."

"Correct."

I sighed under my breath and eased back in my chair. I didn't want anything to do with public enemy number one and now I saw a way out. I frowned and said to Prentice, "Unfortunately, right now I'm moving into a new office, so I'm kind of on a break. If it's urgent like you say, you might want to find someone else. Sorry."

I'm not sure Godfather junior heard a word I said, because he didn't miss a beat. "Mr. Jones, if you know who my father is, and I'm certain you do, then you know on what scale he operates. This could be an enormous opportunity for you."

"Right, I get that but—" I hit the pause button because of the way Prentice's sidekick eyeballed me. Not only was he older, but he was also bigger. An ex–football player was my bet. Seeing his jaw tighten and his hands ball into fists instantly told me they didn't come out to Venice Beach to hear Jackson Jones say no.

"You know what?" I said, changing my tone. "Let's schedule the meeting for tomorrow. I'm guessing Big Ced—sorry, Mr. Willis— likes to sleep in so, I don't know, how about eleven a.m.?"

"He's expecting you now."

I blinked. "Now? You want me to drive there now?"

"No. There's a car waiting around the corner. It's better if you ride with us."

Time stopped briefly. Then I couldn't help myself. I shook my head and laughed.

The two men traded looks, then Prentice said, "Something funny?"

"Yeah. I thought Bogart shit like this only happened in movies."

Prentice, to his credit, wasn't offended. Instead, he chuckled. "Look, my father just wants to talk. Nothing more. You'll be perfectly safe. You have my word."

I don't know why I would believe the word of a gangster, but the dude sounded like he meant it. Also, to be honest, I was damn curious about this whole *urgent matter* business. Lastly, Prentice wasn't kidding about his old man. Cedric Willis wasn't called Big Ced because he was fat or muscular. No, he earned that nickname because everything Big Ced did, legal or illegal, he did, well . . . big. Maybe this would turn out to be a straight-up PI gig with a Big Ced–sized payday. Maybe this truly was an *enormous opportunity*.

"Okay, I'm in," I said, reaching for my iPhone. "Just let me call my partner so she can meet us there."

"There's no need to call Ms. Cunningham," he said. "That's being handled."

I almost laughed at his reference to Mac as *Ms. Cunningham*. He obviously didn't know Mac the way I did.

"Um. When you say *being handled* do you mean like the way you two ran up on me? Just so you know, she isn't as easygoing as I am. I mean, she might even—"

Prentice held up a definitely manicured hand. "We're wasting time. Let's go. My father hates to be kept waiting."

"Sure." I left a tip on the table, then exited the patio and followed them.

For an instant I considered taking off down the boardwalk, but then remembered that I was no longer working alone. I now had a partner to worry about . . . and count on. And she had to be able to count on me. Even if I gave these jokers the slip there was no way to be certain what would happen to Mackenzie.

So, yes, I willingly followed two armed criminals to their car.

There's a popular T-shirt many vendors sell on the Venice boardwalk that warns: *Venice Beach, Where Art Meets Crime.*

Yeah, tell me about it.

Chapter 2

Standing at the base of the steepest hill at Kenneth Hahn Park, I was about to embark on my fifth and final sprint. The panoramic view of LA awaiting me at the top was well worth the grueling workout.

This secluded haven, a favorite of true fitness fanatics, was an ideal spot to get a rigorous workout without having to dart around dog walkers and baby strollers.

The park was also my go-to spot for releasing pent-up frustration. And after a week of dealing with Jackson Jones, my agitation meter was inching into the red zone.

While I was still excited about our joint venture, I was exhausted from our epic battles over everything from office decor to billing rates to the name of our new firm. After a stalemate over whose name would go first, we finally settled on Safe and Sound Investigations. A tad mundane, yet charming in its own right.

I stretched my arms high above my head, took a deep breath, then blasted up the hill like an Olympic sprinter. By the time I reached the top, my lungs were on fire. I bent forward, gripping my thighs for support as I gasped for air.

As I rose, a man leaning against a shiny silver Cadillac Escalade several yards away set off some serious red flags. He was not here for a workout. He was casually dressed in a sport coat over a black T-shirt, but there was nothing casual about his hulking demeanor.

I zeroed in on his white leather tennis shoes, clearly crafted for style rather than function. The emblem on the side looked familiar, but even under duress, I couldn't tell you if the brand was Armani or Adidas. Of course, my snob of a partner would've instantly recognized them and bragged that he had two pairs still in their original shoeboxes sitting in a closet three times the size of my kitchen.

As I kept my focus on the WWE wannabe, the SUV's passenger door opened and a woman emerged. She rounded the car and headed straight for me. Dressed in a black tailored leather blazer, her hair pulled back in a ponytail, she was probably in her midforties, but could've passed for much younger.

I took a step back, letting her know I didn't appreciate people getting in my personal space.

"Can I help you?" I asked.

"My name is Jada." She smiled and extended her hand like she wanted to be my friend.

When I left her hanging, she continued, the smile still in place.

"Ms. Cunningham, my boss would like to hire you for a job," she said.

"I'm off today. Have your boss, whoever he is, call my assistant and set up a meeting."

Before continuing my stroll, I mentally ran through a few Krav Maga moves just in case the pair was looking for trouble. I also surveyed the area. The nearby picnic tables were empty. A handful of walkers were headed toward the bowl-shaped, circular walking path. If something was about to go down, at least there would be witnesses.

"Mackenzie, please wait. My boss is Cedric Willis. He needs to talk to you. Today. Now. We're here to take you to his office."

That stopped me cold. Willis was a man you'd call a respectable criminal. For decades, his network of underworld, political, and financial connections shielded him from any repercussions from his myriad of illegal activities. But despite his scary reputation, that didn't give him the right to summon me to his office like I was one of his underlings.

"Tell your boss I appreciate the gesture," I said with a chuckle, "but I don't accept rides from strangers."

For the first time, Jada dropped her smiley face. "Cedric Willis never accepts no for an answer."

Her tone was menacing now. Still, I remained unfazed.

"Exactly what kind of job does he want to hire me for?"

"I'm not at liberty to say. But I'll get you back here in no time," she said, reverting to friendship mode. "I promise."

"Give me the address. I'll drive myself."

I had no intention of going to meet Willis. Let him make an appointment and come to my office.

"That won't work," she said.

My eyes crisscrossed the immediate area. The walkers I'd seen earlier were gone. If Jada instructed wrestler dude to force me into his car, they might just get away with it. I patted the cell phone in the side pocket of my leggings, wishing it was my .38.

I purposely slowed my breathing and forced myself to think rationally. Snatching women off the street was not Big Ced's MO. It was highly unlikely that they were going to take me to some abandoned warehouse and work me over.

"This is on the up-and-up," she assured me. "Big Ced needs to talk is all."

"So where's this meeting supposed to take place?" I asked as I committed the Escalade's license plate to memory.

"Mr. Willis's office downtown. On Fifth Street."

Strangely, a bit of excitement began to bubble up in my chest. If a mogul like Willis wanted to hire me, the job would probably come with a big paycheck. I'd worked for some seedy people in the past; granted, not on his scale. As long as a gig wouldn't land me in jail or a graveyard, I was usually game. A smile eased across my face. I was going to love showing Jackson up by landing our first big case.

"I'll go with you," I said, pulling my phone from my pocket. "But I have to let my partner know where I'll be."

Just in case he needs to play superhero and rescue me. Jackson would love that.

"No need," Jada replied. "Mr. Jones is already en route."

Whoa. I wasn't sure if that little tidbit was reason for relief or concern. Either way, Jackson should've given me a heads-up.

Jada walked over to the Escalade and swung open the front passenger door. "You can ride shotgun." She flashed me another faux smile.

Ignoring her, I reached for the handle of the back door. I needed to keep an eye on my two escorts.

"I'll go with you," I said, climbing inside, "but I prefer the view from back here."

Chapter 3

JACKSON

Look at this place. Plush. Sleek. Screams success. Now, this is what I'm talking about."

Mac and I were in the reception area, seated side by side on the most comfortable leather sofa my butt had ever met. The ultra-modern decor looked Italian. About as upscale as you can get. A huge, illuminated Willis Worldwide sign loomed over the reception desk, a testament to Big Ced's commitment to living large.

"Seriously?" Mackenzie said, leveling glare Number Nine at me. I had all her sideways looks cataloged. There were twelve in all. Number Nine involved pursed lips and a weary stare. "You're unbelievable."

"Now what?"

There was a receptionist seated a few feet away, so Mackenzie dropped her voice. "We've been kidnapped. That's what."

I chuckled. "Stop it."

"Well, practically." She lowered her voice again. "And now we're about to be face-to-face with a mobster."

"Former mobster."

She hit me with Number Seven, the *yeah, right* sneer.

"We might be in real trouble here and all you can do is admire the office furniture."

"Until we know what this is," I said, "let's just go with it."

"Like we have a choice."

"Bright side. This could be lucrative. I mea—"

"I know. I know. Why do you think I allowed that woman to abduct me?"

I laughed. "Hey, and if this is the mother lode, going top shelf on our office furniture won't be an issue."

"Jackson, I swear, if you mention office furniture again—"

"Excuse me," the receptionist said, rounding her desk. She was pretty and professional, like she belonged on the cover of *Success* magazine. "It'll just be a few minutes more. In the meantime, may I get you something to drink? Coffee? Tea? Water? Or how about a delicious cash-money smoothie?"

Mackenzie and I both made faces.

The receptionist chuckled. "That's what Mr. Willis calls it. It's a green smoothie. Fresh veggies and fruit. Pine nuts. A little acai powder. Would you like one?"

"Sure. Sounds tasty."

The receptionist pivoted her perfect corporate smile to Mac.

Mac shook her head. "No, I'm good."

I nudged her. "Come on, try one. You like healthy stuff."

She hit me with Number Ten, which resembles Nine, but a little spicier. Then Mac turned back to the receptionist. "No, thank you."

"Okay, I'll be right back." With that she disappeared through a side door.

Mackenzie shook her head. "You're just fine with all this, huh?"

"Come on, it might be our last meal."

"Not funny. We need a strategy."

"We need to listen to the details and hope it's not anything too crazy."

"No, I mean an exit strategy," Mackenzie said. "An excuse to refuse the gig if it's too crazy."

I nodded. "Good point. Any ideas?"

"I'm thinking. I'm thinking."

"Me too."

Before we could come up with anything, the receptionist entered a side door carrying the smoothie. It was indeed money green. She handed it to me along with a straw. "Here you go. Tell me what you think?"

I took a sip. It tasted like a cold and frothy garden and was genuinely delicious. "Wow, I love it."

"I knew you would." She returned to her station wearing a satisfied smile.

Mackenzie stared at me as I took another sip.

"Mmmm mmmm." I held out my glass to her. "You really should try some. Just a little sip. Hey, we should get a juicer for our office."

At that moment I added a new glare to the list. Number Thirteen. Nostril flare, micro-twitches of the eye, and I believe I heard knuckles crack. I'm pretty sure Mac would've slapped my cash-money smoothie clear across the reception area if Prentice hadn't suddenly emerged from a pair of double doors.

"Sorry for the wait," he said. As we rose from the sofa, he extended a hand to Mackenzie. "Prentice Willis. Thank you for coming."

Mackenzie only hesitated a second before shaking his hand. "I'd say *you're welcome* but that would be untrue. I will say I'm eager to find out what this is all about."

"Of course. They're ready in the conference room."

"They?" I asked. "I thought we were just meeting your father."

A knowing smile creased Prentice's lips, a smile that I did not like one bit. From the look on Mac's face, she didn't like it either.

"Sorry if I gave you the wrong impression," Prentice said. "Along with my father, there are two other, shall we say, men of significance, eager to meet you both."

Mackenzie got the question out first. "What men? Can we have names?"

"You'll know soon enough." He gestured to the double doors. "Come."

"Wait a minute." I held up my smoothie. "Can I bring this?"

"Better not. My father won't care, but his guests can be a bit . . . unpredictable."

Not liking the sound of that, I took one last sip before setting the drink down on a side table.

Mac whispered out of the corner of her mouth, "Can you please stop acting like we're here for a friendly lunch date?"

"Hey, you need to chill. That was the best smoothie I ever tasted. I hope it's still here when we're done."

Mackenzie rolled her eyes as we followed Prentice through the double doors.

The spacious conference room did exactly what it was designed to do, impress the hell out of anyone who entered. Rich leather furnishings, dual video walls, and a mahogany touchscreen conference table made for an elegant integration of luxury and state-of-the art technology. A floor-to-ceiling picture window spanned the entire length of the room. Although the solar shades were drawn, it was easy to imagine the thirty-three-story-high panorama of downtown Los Angeles ready to be revealed with just the push of a button.

When Mackenzie and I walked in, I kind of expected to see Big Ced enthroned at the head of the conference table, puffing on a huge cigar.

I wasn't even close.

Instead, the balding, white-bearded kingpin, adorned in a sharp three-piece suit, was seated on the long side of the conference table, flanked by two intimidating-looking men. One was white, the other Hispanic.

I recognized Big Ced's scary bookends instantly. I knew Mackenzie did as well by the way she furtively glanced at me with a look I'd never seen before. This one screamed, *holy shit.*

Holy shit was right.

The curly-headed white man on Big Ced's left was well fed and pushing sixty. He wore a blue tracksuit, thick framed glasses that magnified shrewd eyes, and on his left hand an honest-to-god pinkie ring. His name was Yaron Bioff, head of the Jewish mob.

The other man, in his forties, was the youngest of the trio. He sported a designer embroidered hoodie, a thick tattooed neck adorned with a small fortune in gold chains, and a chilling titanium stare. His name was Mateo Meza, top dog in the Mexican mob.

Life sure is crazy. One minute I'm sipping coffee on the beach, the next Mackenzie and I are standing before three of the most dangerous men on the west coast. These guys were big-time rivals. So why were they sitting around a table acting like they were about to break bread?

Registering our baffled expressions, Prentice smiled and said, "Do I need to make formal introductions or are we all good?"

"Nah, I'm good," I muttered, quieter than I wanted to admit.

"Same," Mackenzie said, nodding her head.

"Excellent." Big Ced's voice was deep, bordering on regal, but unlike his son, he had to work to keep the street out of his vocabulary. "Go on, sit. Please."

Mac and I settled into plush high-back chairs, directly across from the three men.

"Before we begin," he continued, "my associates and I want to thank you for coming on such short notice."

"Yes," Yaron Bioff said.

Mateo Meza just barely nodded his head.

Big Ced went on. "I heard how you two cracked that politician case several weeks back. It was all over the news. Damned impressive."

Mackenzie and I both said thank you, but what I really wanted to say was *get to the point already so I can get my ass up out of here.* I'd bet anything my partner was thinking the same thing.

"So, of course," he continued, "when a certain situation presented itself that required a particular brand of outside help, I told my colleagues here about you. We quickly came to the agreement that Jackson Jones and Mackenzie Cunningham are our best chance of resolving this situation. And that's why you're sitting here now."

Mackenzie and I both flashed respectful smiles, then Mackenzie found the nerve to say what I was thinking. "We appreciate your confidence, Mr. Willis, we really do. But we're going to need details to determine if this job is even right for us."

I literally held my breath.

Yaron Bioff and Mateo Meza threw glances at Big Ced.

Big Ced ignored them. Instead, he just smiled at Mackenzie for about a second too long, then finally said, "Absolutely. But first I should emphasize something. Typically, me and the gentlemen beside me would prefer not to cross paths. Bad for business. The fact that we're all seated at the same table, essentially acting as one, should give you both some idea of the level of urgency we're dealing with."

Yaron Bioff bobbed his head. "Willis is right. It's bad. Extremely urgent."

Mateo Meza, his eyes somehow locked on both of us, just said one word. "Sí."

I didn't know about Mackenzie, but my heart was beating faster than a hummingbird's. Suddenly, I didn't want any details. I didn't want to hear another word.

Big Ced leaned forward slightly. "Do you both understand?"

Mackenzie and I nodded stiffly.

Despite the tension bearing down on me, what happened next almost made me burst out laughing.

Prentice picked up a small remote control from the conference table and said, "I've prepared a PowerPoint presentation that will explain everything."

Mackenzie and I couldn't help trading astounded looks. These guys were acting as if this were a corporate board meeting.

"Don't worry," Prentice said. "It's quite brief." He hit play. The recessed lighting dimmed and the humongous video wall came to life.

The image of a fiftyish white man driving a burgundy convertible Bentley filled the screen. His long white hair tossed by the wind. His face aglow with a huge twinkle-eyed smile. This dude literally looked like the happiest man in the world.

"This is Vincent Keane," Prentice said. "Lawyer, accountant, computer coder, and most important, a fucking con man."

A mug shot of a much younger Keane filled the screen.

"This mug shot was taken twenty-five years ago, when he was just cutting his teeth. Improving his game before going big league. Roughly ten years ago, Mr. Keane utilized his assortment of skills to acquire some influential clients and so-called friends."

Photos of Keane with Big Ced, Mateo Meza, and Yaron Bioff flashed on-screen.

"Vincent Keane then used these relationships to steal and compile highly confidential information about my father, Mr. Bioff, and Mr. Meza. Information that could prove very damaging if it fell into the wrong hands . . . like, say, the district attorney."

The image of a suited middle-aged man standing proudly before an American flag filled the video wall. I didn't know for sure, but I guessed he was the current LA district attorney.

"For almost a decade Mr. Keane has used this advantage to blackmail the men in this room for enormous amounts of money, in monthly installments, no less. Now, you might be wondering, how does Keane get away with it? These are powerful men. Men of influence. Why couldn't they stop him?"

If Keane was as clever as he sounded, I knew how he did it: he had insurance in case they tried to make him disappear.

A close-up of Vincent Keane wearing a knowing smirk filled the screen.

Prentice continued. "Keane had dirt that he used as insurance."

I mentally patted myself on the back.

"Keane made it clear that if anything ever happened to him there was a process in place to ensure that damaging information about us ended up on the DA's desk."

For some reason I raised my hand before speaking—maybe it was the formality of the PowerPoint. "This is all very interesting, but how could Mackenzie and I help you solve this problem?"

"I'll show you," Prentice said, then he pressed a button on the remote.

Images of a major car accident flashed on the video wall. A smashed-to-hell burgundy Bentley strewn across Pacific Coast Highway. Vincent Keane, covered in blood, being pulled from the wreck on a stretcher. He did not look good.

I was relieved to see that Mackenzie also raised her hand. "So, he's dead?"

Prentice shook his head. "Not yet. Currently Keane's hospitalized at UCLA Medical Center in Westwood. Intensive care. Hanging by a thread on life support. The doctors give him less than a week. They say it's a miracle he's still alive. And that miracle is an opportunity for us."

Prentice killed the video wall. When the conference room lights returned to their original intensity, Big Ced leaned forward over the table. "Do you two get it now? When that motherfucker dies, we're done." He gestured to the men beside him. "All three of us. Finished. We can't let that happen."

Bioff shook his curly head. "No, no, no. Absolutely not."

"Fuck no!" Meza pounded his fist on the conference table, causing Mac and me to flinch.

Prentice jumped in. "We need you two to locate Vincent's stash before he dies, then return that stash to us so we can destroy it. Thumb drives, paper files, microfilm, format doesn't matter. What does matter is that you get it all and nothing reaches the DA. And you'll need this."

Prentice picked up a manila folder and set it down in front of me and Mackenzie.

"It's everything we have on Keane. Addresses. Friends. Family. Enemies. The works. There's a check in there too. Take a look."

I opened the manila folder and slid out a bank check with lots of zeroes.

"That's fifty grand to start." Prentice said. "Once you're done, you get another one hundred and fifty. Sound good?"

Mackenzie and I just sat there staring at that fat check, each other, and all those intense stares focused on us. Waiting.

"So, tell me." Big Ced's voice was disturbingly calm. "Do we have a deal . . . or not?"

I could tell from Mackenzie's eyes that she and I were on the same page. To hell with all that money, we wanted nothing to do with this fucked-up version of *The Godfather*.

"Sounds like trouble," Mackenzie said. "Big trouble."

Big Ced sat back in his chair, a look of displeasure slowly spreading across his face.

"Are you kidding?" I stepped in, snatched the check, and tucked it in my pocket. "This is clearly an offer we can't refuse. Am I right, Mr. Willis?"

Big Ced held me with a razor-thin smile, then finally said, "My son forgot one thing. Something very important. There is to be absolutely no police involvement. You got that?"

I nodded. Mackenzie did not. I could tell from the tightness of her jawline that she was steaming inside. "We got it," I said.

"Good. Now get to work. The clock's ticking."

Chapter 4

MACKENZIE

Jackson and I were both mindfully mute as the Escalade inched down Washington Boulevard. It was hours before rush hour, but you wouldn't know it from all the cars on the street.

Instead of being taken back to our individual pickup spots, Jackson—without consulting me, of course—directed our driver, the Hulk Hogan wannabe, to drop us off at our new office in Culver City.

"We can Uber to my place from the office," he told me after we climbed into the back seat, still reeling from our multi-mobster face-off. "Then I can take you to the park to pick up your Jeep."

Gazing out the window, I silently seethed over the predicament we were in. These were not the kind of clients we should be associating with. Jackson, however, seemed to be quite pleased with that fifty grand check tucked away in his wallet—he kept sneaking glances at it on our ride back. I wanted to snatch it from his greedy little fingers and hurl it out of the window.

I managed to suppress my anger until the second we stepped into our nearly empty office, which was scattered with unpacked boxes.

"If we're going to do business together," I said, locking my arms across my chest, "we need to do business *together.* We should've asked for a few minutes to discuss their offer. But you just grabbed that check like a hungry hyena."

Jackson scrunched up his face, then made a dramatic show of looking around the office. He even picked up a box to look underneath it.

"What are you doing?" I asked. "What are you looking for?"

"I'm looking for Mackenzie Cunningham because *you* are not her. I can't believe what you just said. *Discuss their offer?* Are you kidding me? We were sitting across from three men who consider murder a peaceful pastime. There was nothing to discuss. We had no choice. You think I *wanted* to take this job?"

The harsh reality of Jackson's words jolted me. We were trapped in a corner with no viable escape route. I plopped down on one of the boxes and pressed my palms to my face.

"You're right," I said, my exasperation clear. "You're absolutely right. I'm sorry."

Jackson immediately pulled his phone from his pocket and shoved it in my face. "Could you please repeat that? I'm certain you'll never utter those words again, so I'd like to have a recording I can listen to over and over again."

I glared up at him. "I'm not in the mood for your jokes. We need to figure out how we're going to get out of this."

Jackson rubbed his forehead, opened one of the folding chairs, and fell into it. "I'm not sure we can."

"We need to go to the police."

Jackson dramatically swung his head from side to side. "No way. You heard what they said."

"I'm not talking about officially. We both have contacts with LAPD. The FBI too. Let's find someone we can trust and get some advice on the down low about how we should proceed. We can't go this alone."

"Those guys probably have people on the inside. That wouldn't be a wise move."

"Okay then, tell me what *would* be a wise move?"

Jackson locked eyes with me. The fear and frustration in his eyes mirrored mine.

"We could take the money and run," he said, suddenly breaking into a mischievous smile. "Fifty grand would go a long way in the Dominican Republic. We could kick back on a white sandy beach and sip piña coladas all day."

"Please stop playing around," I chided him. "This is not the time for that."

"Yes, it is. Because I've got nothing."

I stared across the room at my handsome partner, a man I initially loathed, a feeling that gradually transformed into admiration. Despite our frequent sparring, I came to like him. A lot. We'd had some trying times over the past few months, including being on the run for our lives. I wasn't ready to relive those terrifying moments. But admittedly, if I had to, I'd feel safer doing it with Jackson by my side.

He hopped up and started opening boxes. "Sitting around moping won't help either. Let's get cracking on figuring out how we're going to solve this case. Which box has my laptop?"

"How would I know that? I didn't pack up your stuff."

All of my boxes were identified with neatly typed labels describing their contents. Jackson's mishmash of boxes were unlabeled and weren't even taped shut.

"Well, if you help me look for it, I'll—"

A thunderous pounding suddenly rattled the small office. Before we could react, the door flew open and two men in suits barged inside.

"What the hell?" Jackson said.

The men simultaneously flashed their LAPD detective badges.

"Our boss wants a word with you. Now."

Chapter 5

JACKSON

I guess this room's decor is like your dream space," I said, gazing around the interrogation room.

Mackenzie glared at me. "Stop being ridiculous."

"Am I? Steel desk and chairs, bare walls, cheap little trash bin. Efficiency up the wazoo."

"I said simple," Mackenzie said, "not . . . institutional."

"Wow."

"Wow, what?"

"Look at us. We're actually having a calm conversation about office furniture."

Mackenzie shrugged. "Gotta keep ourselves occupied somehow. I mean, we've been sitting here forever."

Mackenzie and I were crammed into an interrogation room on the third floor of LAPD Headquarters. The detectives who bull-dozed their way into our office refused to tell us who their boss was or why he wanted to talk to us. Almost certainly it was connected to our breakfast meeting with the legion of doom, but the two ro-bocops who brought us in stuck to their programming. They just tossed us into this broom closet and told us to sit tight. That was almost an hour ago. Actually, the long wait didn't surprise me one bit. Letting detainees sweat before a grilling was standard police procedure. What did surprise me was that they'd try that bullshit on me. They had to know that I used to wear a badge. Maybe it was the fact that I'd turned in my corrupt partner that rubbed them the wrong way. Then again, maybe the make-'em-bake routine was all for Mackenzie's benefit. Why try to wring information from a former cop when there might be an easier mark?

But they'd seriously underestimated my new partner. Even though we were alone, Mackenzie knew not to mention anything about Big Ced and company. The two-way mirrored walls, always seen in movies, went out decades ago, replaced by high-definition video cameras and hypersensitive microphones. Mackenzie knew as well as I did that every move we made and every word we uttered was probably being monitored. So, of course we kept it light and entertaining for our audience.

"You know," Mackenzie said, "I get your whole thing about wanting our workplace to radiate success, but flashy furniture doesn't do that. Flashy projects . . . unseriousness."

I chuckled. "First, *unseriousness* is not a word. Second, I never said flashy. I said stylish, elegant, plush."

"*Unseriousness* is definitely a word," Mackenzie said, "Look it up. And those other words are just another way of saying flashy."

"Well, if *unseriousness* is a word, it's definitely a flashy word."

"Very cute."

As if on cue, just as Mackenzie uttered those words, the interrogation room door swung open, and Michael Ealy walked in. Of course, it wasn't really the heartthrob actor that millions of women fantasized about, but it was close. He was tall, light-skinned, with creamy green eyes and a clean-shaven square jaw worthy of a superhero. His athletic-fit blue suit showcased his gym-chiseled form.

The only things distinguishing this dude from a male model were the sidearm and the gold shield attached to his belt.

"I apologize for the wait," he said, his tone formal and concise. "I'm Lieutenant Mark Gooden." He shook my hand first. His grip was firm and confident, underscored by a faint whiff of Dior Sauvage. A classic. He had to be the best-smelling cop in Los Angeles.

When the detective extended his hand to Mackenzie, I instantly noticed that something was off. During our handshake Lieutenant Gooden's expression was professional, bordering on stern. But when he shook hands with Mackenzie, he flashed a perfect smile and, along with a lingering gaze, held on to her hand a tad longer than necessary. Oh, it was subtle, but it was definitely there.

If Mackenzie picked up on any of this, she didn't show her cards.

Gooden sat down directly across from us. "I guess you're wondering why you're here."

"You guessed right," I said.

"I head up LAPD's organized crime unit. Does that help?"

He waited for Mac and me to react.

We gave him zip.

He sighed. "I know about your meeting this morning with Willis, Bioff, and Meza. What I don't know is what that meeting was about." He waited again.

His interrogation technique was on point. I knew from my time on the force that giving interviewees an opportunity to talk themselves into prison was straight out of the textbook. Unfortunately for him we weren't falling for it.

Finally getting the picture, Lieutenant Gooden changed tactics. He chuckled and said, "Look, let's keep this friendly, okay? I won't treat you like dopes and I'd appreciate the same courtesy. Deal?"

Mackenzie and I nodded but remained silent.

"The top three names on our enemies list having a sit-down

is quite rare. Never happens. Now it appears this occurred so that they could meet with a couple of local private investigators. Why? What was that meeting about? What would those three want with you two?"

"Lieutenant Gooden," I said. "As I'm sure you know, the *private* part of private investigators means just that. Our work is confidential. Sorry."

"I see," he said. "So they wanted to hire you two for a job."

"He didn't say that," Mackenzie jumped in. "And we can't confirm that."

"Right," he said, nodding. "So did you accept this job?"

"Also confidential," I said.

"Considering the clients, I'll assume that's a yes."

"You're making a lot of assumptions," Mackenzie said.

"I'll also assume you were strongly advised not to talk to the police. Am I correct?"

I had to hand it to Lieutenant Gooden. He wasn't just a pretty face. He was sharp. Probably top of his class at the academy.

"If you believe you have all the answers," Mackenzie said, "why keep asking questions?"

"Exactly," I chimed in. "Can we go now?"

Lieutenant Gooden crossed his arms and leaned back in his chair. "Look, I like you two. FYI, when you took down that senator's wife, a couple of connected lowlifes went down with her. So, in a way, you did my unit a favor." Then he smiled at Mackenzie. "And, Ms. Cunningham, your interview on *Good Day LA*? Impressive. Your knowledge of the case. The way you broke it all down. That was really something to see."

Mackenzie smiled back. "Thank you. I appreciate that."

What the hell? Either Mackenzie had been secretly taking acting lessons or she looked genuinely flattered.

I said to Lieutenant Gooden, "You know, I was part of that TV interview too. I was sitting right next to Mackenzie. I even answered a few questions."

"Yes, I know. You were good too."

"Gee, thanks."

"To be honest with you, Mr. Jones, you don't have a lot of friends in this building, but there's one sitting right in front of you." He leaned forward and dropped his voice. "Between you and me, I hate that *blue wall* nonsense. It took courage to do what you did. I respect that. Really."

I couldn't tell if Gooden was jazzing me or serious, but his words did make me feel a little something. This dude really was good. Giving him the benefit of the doubt, I said, "Thanks for that."

"Sure thing."

"Look, I'm sure Mackenzie would agree that you seem like an all-right guy, but we still can't tell you anything about that meeting."

"Come on," he urged. "Give me something. Anything. Let us help you. What's said in this room won't get back to Willis and the others. You both have my word."

Mackenzie and I traded looks. We were in deep, so cooperating with Gooden and his team was tempting as hell. But the police could only do so much. They had to play the game by rules the other side didn't abide by. No, the risk was too high. Mac and I were going to have to scratch our way out of this mess on our own.

As if Mackenzie could read my thoughts, we shook our heads simultaneously. "We can't do it," I said. "Sorry."

Lieutenant Gooden sat upright in his chair and his face changed. He went from affable savior to cold adversary in the blink of an eye. "All right," he said. "Since you refuse to talk you need to listen carefully. You're out of your league and you'll probably get yourselves killed. And even if you do come out on the other side of whatever this is, there's still me to deal with. Willis and his buddies are experts at insulating themselves, but you two, not so much. If you're caught up in anything involving those thugs, I'm going to find out and send you to prison for a long time. Understood?"

Damn, not a bad little speech. Made my pulse quicken and everything. I could see Mackenzie taking a breath to settle herself as well.

"We got it," I said. "Are we free to go?"

And just like that Lieutenant Gooden was flashing that toothpaste commercial smile again. Our friend, who liked us so much, was back. "Sure," he said. "Take an Uber back and send me the receipt. I'll make sure you're reimbursed. Thanks again for coming in."

As Mackenzie and I stood up he said, "Wait. Almost forgot." Then he pulled a business card out of his pocket and handed it to Mackenzie. "If you change your mind, or if you just want to talk. Call me."

Was it my imagination or was there a bit of suave emphasis on the words *call me*? Like some kind of Jedi mind trick. The care with which Mackenzie slid that card into her pocket told me I was onto something.

"Hey, Lieutenant," I said. "Could I get one of those cards too?"

He made a face. "Sorry, that was my last one. You two take care of yourselves."

As Mackenzie and I walked out of that interrogation room, I knew one thing for certain. Lieutenant Mark Gooden, head of the LAPD organized crime unit, wanted to catch my new partner in more ways than one.

Chapter 6

MACKENZIE

Whehen we reentered our office, it was as if someone had waved a magic wand, converting it from a cluttered jumble of boxes into a functional, inviting workspace.

Instead of chaos, the office now exuded a sense of calm. Two glass-top desks were symmetrically positioned opposite each other, with our respective laptops sitting squarely in the middle. Behind each desk, a high-back leather chair the color of melted caramel awaited us. All of our boxes were neatly stacked just below a large, vibrant abstract painting which took up most of the north wall. The six-foot majesty palm sitting in the corner was so lifelike, I walked over to touch it just to make sure it wasn't.

I stole a glance at Jackson, only to find him glaring at me.

"Did you order furniture without telling me?" he demanded.

"Of course not. I was assuming you did this to surprise me." I eased into one of the chairs. "I love it."

"Of course you do." Jackson ran a finger along the smooth edge of the desk across from mine. "I'm sorry, but this is a long way from what I had in mind. This must be Nadine's doing. I'm going to strangle her."

As if on cue, Jackson's cousin and faithful assistant rushed into the office and made a beeline for me.

"Welcome, girlfriend! I'm so excited to be working for you." She pulled me into a bear hug. "We're going to have big fun."

"Excuse me," Jackson said. "You work for *us*."

Nadine dismissively waved her hand at him.

"The office looks great," I told her.

Nadine was an absolute delight. We'd clicked the second we met.

"Who told you to buy this stuff?" Jackson barked at her.

"Puh-leeze," she said, rolling her eyes. "I didn't *buy* anything. I know how picky you are. The guy who manages the office next door has a crush on me. He was about to turn this rental furniture in early even though he won't get a refund. So I convinced him to let us borrow it until his contract is up at the end of the month."

"Without asking me?" Jackson said, still perturbed.

"Look," Nadine said, not one bit cowed by Jackson's gruffness, "I did you a favor. You guys get to use this stuff for the next three weeks. I figure that's enough time for y'all to reach a truce in the furniture wars."

"Great idea," I said, high-fiving her.

Jackson just stared at us. "I got a feeling you two are going to be ganging up on me."

Nadine winked. "Count on it."

As she walked out, Jackson begrudgingly slumped into the chair behind his desk. I could tell from his expression that he was surprised by how much he liked it.

"Nice, huh?" I said.

"No," he grumbled, pointing at the wall. "And that so-called artwork looks like it came from HomeGoods. So don't get used to it. Let's get to work."

"Whatever," I said. "Let's take a look at the file they gave us on Vincent Keane."

I stood over Jackson's shoulder and examined the folder along with him.

It contained more photos of Keane as well as some short profiles of the people closest to him—his daughter, ex-wife, and an escort he'd been seeing for some time. There were vague references to the deals he'd made with the three crime families, but no real details other than the payments: fifty grand a month from each family. I wondered what other cars he owned besides that Bentley.

"Wow," I said. "This guy was definitely shady."

"Shady and ballsy," Jackson said. "He must've had a death wish to fuck with these dudes. I wonder exactly what he's holding over their heads?"

"I don't know and I don't wanna know," I said. "Let's just find the evidence, hand it over, collect our dough, and be on our way."

"Look at the bright side," Jackson said. "Three good things happened today. First, we're going to make two hundred thousand dollars. Not bad for the first case for our new agency."

"Yeah," I said, "if they actually pay us."

"They will. It's an honor thing."

"They're criminals," I pointed out.

"You've never heard of honor among thieves?"

"We're not thieves. So what's the second good thing that happened today?"

"We got free *temporary* office furniture," Jackson said. "So we don't have to sit on folding chairs until we get some premium furniture in here."

I smiled. "I'm betting that in a month, you're not going to want to part with this stuff."

"Ain't gonna happen."

"Whatever. And the third thing?" I asked.

"It looks like you might've found true love. I couldn't believe the way Lieutenant Goodie sat there eyeing you like a piece of meat."

"His name is Gooden, not Goodie. And he wasn't eyeing me."

"Yes, he was. And when he handed you his business card and said *call me*, the lust in his voice had nothing to do with business."

"Awww," I said in a mocking voice, "are you upset because he didn't have a business card for you too? There's no need for you to be jealous."

"I'm not jealous."

"Yes, he is," Nadine yelled from the hallway.

"Nobody's talking to you," Jackson fired back. "We're wasting time. Where should we start?"

"Let's check out Keane's house," I said.

Jackson scratched his jaw. "I doubt he'd be stupid enough to keep something so important at his home."

"You're probably right, but you never know."

Jackson closed the folder and stood up. "Then I guess we're going to Malibu."

Chapter 7

JACKSON

Moje láska, it is so wonderful to hear your voice."

"It's great to hear yours as well. You're on speaker, so don't say anything mean about Mackenzie."

Mac and I were cruising west on the PCH in my red AMG E-Class, en route to Vincent Keane's house in Malibu. Although my Mercedes is a convertible, the top was up because Ms. Cunningham hates all things fun.

"Hey, Rox," Mackenzie called out from the passenger seat.

"*Můje anděl*," Roxanna's Czech-accented voice chimed from my car's sixteen-speaker Burmester surround-sound system. "How are you, darling?"

"You know what they say, any day aboveground is a good day."

"To be honest, that does not sound good at all."

Mackenzie chuckled. "I guess I'm being a little dramatic."

"Guess? Why guess? What are you not telling me?"

"Mac has a new boyfriend," I said, jumping in. "Lieutenant Mark Gooden of the LAPD. A real hunk."

Mackenzie shot me glare Number Four. "Would you stop?"

"What? I can't talk about your boyfriend?"

"You're such a child sometimes."

Of course, that was my cue to begin singing. "Mark and Mackenzie sitting in a tree. K.I.S.S.I.N.—"

"I'm going to punch you. I swear."

"Oooo, yes," Roxanna said. "You are right. Lieutenant Gooden is very sexy man."

"Wait. You know him?" Mackenzie asked.

Roxanna chuckled. "Do you forget who I am? His photos, employment records, credit reports, medical history, everything. I have it all here on my lovely monitors."

Realizing her mistake, Mackenzie winced. "Of course you do."

Roxanna Novakova wasn't merely a tattoo-addicted beauty, she was also a world-class hacker. In the movies and comic books they'd call her "the guy in the chair," a tech-savvy individual who sits at a keyboard all day providing vital information to superheroes or detectives in the field. Since day one of my PI career, Roxy, armed with a bleeding-edge computer system, has always been my girl in the chair. Back when I was an ex-cop pursuing a career as a masseur, Roxy was just a client, my best client actually. Those lucrative house calls quickly evolved into a feverish sexual affair, then eventually our relationship evolved into something even stronger. Deep friendship. Even after the lust waned, the friendship continued to burn bright, and still does to this day.

"I hoped for you and Jackson love connection," Roxanna said, "but this new boyfriend, this Gooden, I do much approve."

"Don't listen to him," Mackenzie said. "Gooden's nothing to me, except a jerk trying to throw us in jail."

"Jail? Why do you say this?"

"It's a long story, Rox," I said. "No time to go into detail. Right now we need your help on a new case."

Chapter 8

MACKENZIE

I listened as Jackson began telling Roxanna how we needed her help. Without, of course, divulging anything about the dangerous men who'd hired us. I wondered, though, if she'd eventually find out that information on her own.

"There's an accountant slash lawyer named Vincent Keane. Currently comatose at UCLA Medical Center," Jackson began. "We need you to do a deep dive on this guy. Particular focus on possible safety deposit boxes, storage facilities, offshore accounts. Anywhere he could hide something important. I know you're always busy but we're really in a spot. We need this ASAP. Can you help?"

"Of course," Roxanna replied without hesitation. "Anything for you and Mackenzie, *můj miláček*. This you know."

"Thanks, Rox. Our client is loaded. We'll settle up after the case is closed if that's okay."

"I don't need your money. But my back is killing me. I would love one of your wonderful massages. Your long, sexy fingers do magic to my body. I need full treatment."

"You got it. Full treatment."

I rolled my eyes and made a face at Jackson.

"Get your mind out of the gutter," he said. "My massages are legit."

"Yes. Very legit," she purred.

I could almost see Roxanna's dreamy smile.

"TMI," I said. "Let's get back to business."

"No, wait," Roxanna said. "You give two massages and you have deal."

"Deal," Jackson quickly agreed.

"One for me and one for Mackenzie."

"Wait. What?" I jumped in.

Roxanna sighed. "You much stressed, Mackenzie, you must have Jackson's full treatment. That is my price or no information. Good, yes?"

"All right, fine," I said hesitantly, wishing I could wipe the smug smile off Jackson's face.

"Wonderful. Now I get to work. *Na shledanou*." And the call went dead.

Jackson couldn't help chuckling as I gave him a puzzled glare. "What did I just agree to?"

"She was pretty clear. The full treatment."

"And what's that exactly?"

"Don't worry. You'll find out."

"Just tell me."

"Okay. The full treatment is a treatment that is . . . full."

"You are such a jerk."

He was still laughing as we took the next exit onto a winding two-lane road that snaked its way up into the Malibu Hills.

"Check out these amazing cribs," Jackson said. "Every house up here has a view of the Pacific Ocean and an eight-figure price tag."

"You're such a wannabe," I said.

"Hey, a brother can dream, can't he?"

Vincent Keane's house was just as fabulous as the homes of his neighbors. After ascending a steep private driveway, we parked in the shadow of a modern, all-white, boxy, three-story mansion that looked more like a museum than someone's home. Keane had to be siphoning some serious coin from his underworld benefactors to afford this place.

"You see," Jackson said. "I knew it."

"What?" I asked.

"We've been lied to. Crime *does* pay."

I could only laugh in agreement.

We climbed out of the Mercedes and started up the walk. Jackson had already laid out our plan. First, we'd ring the doorbell. Because Keane lived alone, we didn't expect anyone to be home. Once that was confirmed, we'd pick the lock and give the place a quick once-over. If our lock-picking failed, we'd just kick in a back window. Of course this might set off an alarm, but statistically speaking, 25 percent of homes don't have alarm systems, and of those that do, half are not regularly turned on. Those were not good odds, but that's what we had to work with.

When Jackson and I reached the welcome mat, which read Welcome-ish, we were greeted by a sight that we had not anticipated.

The front door was ajar.

So much for lockpicks and alarms.

Anyone who's watched TV or movies knows an ajar door usually means there's something bad on the other side.

I shot Jackson a look as he drew his .38 and held it ready.

I pulled my gun as well and slowly pushed open the door. "Hello! Anyone here? Hello!"

There was no answer, but the sight before us said enough. Someone had beaten us to Vincent Keane's place.

The interior of the house was trashed. Designer furniture smashed and ripped to shreds. Electronics gutted. A grand piano pummeled into a black lacquered wood pile. Sections of marble flooring pulled up. Gaping holes in the walls. Even holes in the ceilings.

Our trip was a complete waste of time. There was nothing left for us to find here.

Five minutes later we were speeding along Pacific Coast Highway in the opposite direction, headed to our next planned stop, Vincent Keane's office in Beverly Hills.

Prentice had made it clear that his people had made no attempt to search for Keane's stash. They were worried, and rightly so, that someone could be watching on Keane's behalf, ready to FedEx the DA if anything looked out of whack. That meant someone else was searching for the information. And judging by how that someone had ransacked Keane's house, they didn't care about being noticed.

"Let's call Prentice," Jackson said.

I pulled out my phone and dialed his number, but it went straight to voicemail. "Should I call back and leave a message?"

"No," Jackson said. "We'll try later."

Right now Jackson and I were in full agreement. Prentice needed to know ASAP that the hunt he'd hired us for had turned into a race.

Chapter 9

JACKSON

You think it's possible Prentice lied to us?" Mackenzie asked as we continued our drive to Keane's office.

"Why lie and let us waste time looking under rocks they'd already turned over? No, someone else is on the same scent for sure."

"Makes sense," she said. "Information like that is priceless."

I nodded. "After we check Keane's office, we'll try Prentice again."

"I know the chances are slim, but what if the info really was hidden in Keane's house?" Her face was filled with worry. "What if somebody already found it?"

"I doubt it. That demolition job looked like the work of someone seriously pissed off. Someone who came up empty. Let's just hope they haven't beaten us to Keane's office as well."

We rode in silence for a long stretch, then Mackenzie suddenly turned to me with an earnest look on her face. "Let's make a deal."

"A deal? I'm listening."

"It's simple. I'll let you put down the top if you tell me what the full treatment is."

"Uh . . . Nope." My lips angled into a smile. "Some things you just don't need to know."

I broke out into full laughter as she fumed.

When the car's navigation system announced that we had arrived at our destination, we were greeted by another surprise.

A fenced-in vacant lot.

We found a security guard at a business across the street who told us the enormous turn-of-the-century building in which Keane had rented office space had fallen to the wrecking ball over a year ago.

Turns out Prentice had provided us with outdated information, which instantly made me question the validity of everything else in that manila folder. You'd think gangsters would keep better records of the people they wanted dead.

While the car idled, Mackenzie made another call to Prentice, which again went to voicemail. That dude had some nerve hiring us for a twisted scavenger hunt then disappearing off the face of the earth. Then again, maybe something was wrong. Maybe Vincent Keane really was dumb enough to hide the info in his house, and now it was gone. Maybe the who's who of the underworld were scrambling like roaches and had forgotten all about Mackenzie Cunningham and Jackson Jones.

We called Roxanna back, hoping she could provide us with an address for Keane's new office, but there was no new office.

"He moved out of that building almost two years ago," Roxanna said over the car's speaker system. "And after that, he worked from home."

"Okay," I said. "What about storage spaces? Safety deposit boxes? Anything like that?"

"No. I have found nothing yet. *Miláčku*, it might help, yes, if you tell me exactly what you're looking for."

Mackenzie and I frowned at each other, silently agreeing that sharing that poisonous info with Roxanna was a very bad idea. We were not about to put her life in danger.

"Roxy," I said, "you know I love you to death, but we can't tell you. You're just going to have to trust us on this."

"Jackson, I do not like how this sounds. No. But of course I trust you, *moje láska*. Of course."

"Thanks, Rox."

Mackenzie snapped her fingers. "Hey, what about Keane's car? The Bentley from the accident. Maybe he kept something in there."

I wagged my head. "I don't know. That sounds like a bigger stretch than the house idea. But, hey, what else we got?"

"Exactly," Mackenzie said. "That car was a total wreck and it wasn't at his house. I'll bet it's at a tow yard."

"I bet you're right," I said. "Roxy, can you do a quick—"

"Hush. I am already on it."

The impossibly rapid clicking of a keyboard filled the car. Mac looked as astounded as I was. *Can anyone really type that fast?*

"Found it," Roxanna said. "Pacific Coast Tow Service on Twelfth Street in Santa Monica. And this car scheduled for crushing first thing tomorrow."

"Damn," I said. "Then we better get over there now."

"Not necessary," Roxanna said. "There is a list of the personal items recovered from the car. Wallet, umbrella, briefcase, cell phone, vape pen—"

"Stop," I said. "The cell phone sounds promising. There could be all kinds of information in there."

"There is nothing," Roxy said.

"How do you know that?"

"I sifted his cellular data already."

"When? You just found out about the damn phone."

Roxanna chuckled. "*Hloupý*, everything's faster now with AI. This you do not know?"

"Hold on," I said. "Roxy, you said there was a briefcase, right?"

"Correct. A Hermès carbon-fiber briefcase. It is quite nice."

"It's also pretty thin," I said. "Very, very thin. It wouldn't hold much. Anyway, Keane would have to be crazy to keep that info on him."

"Nobody uses paper anymore," Mackenzie said. "It's probably on a thumb drive. A nearly indestructible briefcase would be a good place to keep it."

"Maybe," I said.

"Maybe the briefcase has a secret compartment. Or maybe there's something in it that'll give us a clue where to look next."

I considered this possibility. "Can't argue with that. Roxy, is Keane's briefcase still at the tow yard?"

"No," Roxanna said. "It was sent to the UCLA hospital. It is with Mr. Keane's personal effects."

"Not good," I said. "Personal effects are usually kept in the patient's room. Keane's in the ICU, the most eyeballed part of any hospital. Even with Roxy's help we'd never get close to it."

"Unfortunately," Roxanna said. "This is truth. Maybe I get you past security cameras and electronic locks, but people, no."

I frowned. "Searching Keane's briefcase isn't a bad idea, but we can't get to him as long as he's in the ICU."

"Not so fast," Mackenzie said. "I know someone who might be able to help us."

Chapter 10

This is a pretty swanky place," Jackson said, swiveling his head around the waiting room of my brother's office in a high-rise medical building off Westwood Boulevard. "Very impressive."

Of course, Jackson would be impressed. My brother, Winston, a well-regarded orthopedic surgeon, definitely enjoyed the finer things in life. He'd hired an interior decorator and her work showed. Blue suede club chairs, soft beige walls, seductive lighting, and a glass-top coffee table complete with fresh flowers.

It was almost one o'clock. Winston reserved Tuesday mornings for surgery, so the waiting room was empty.

"Now that's what you call art," Jackson said, pointing across the room. "I bet that cost him a pretty penny. Not like that crap in our office."

I shook my head. "Complete waste of money. Knowing my brother and his taste, it scares me to imagine how much it cost."

"I still can't believe your brother is actually going to tell us how to sneak into Keane's hospital room. He's got too much on the line to be helping us break the law."

"If we do manage to get into Keane's room," I said, "we won't be breaking the law, just hospital policy. I'd never put my brother in that kind of position. Winston did his residency at UCLA Medical Center, so he knows that hospital like the back of his hand. If there's a way for us to get into Keane's room, he'll know how to do it."

"If you say so. I just think—"

At that moment, the door to the left of the receptionist's desk burst open and my brother lumbered into the lobby.

"My man!" Winston said, extending his hand to Jackson, his smile taking up half his face. "I've been dying to meet you. Congrats on your new business venture. Any brother who can go head-to-head with my knucklehead sister has to be a stone-cold gladiator."

They did the whole Black-man-handshake thing, all the way down to the touching of the fingertips.

"I've heard nothing but good things about you," Jackson lied.

My brother and only sibling is my best friend, but I hadn't shared much about him with Jackson. Despite our private school upbringing and our very prim and proper parents, Winston liked to brandish the persona of a brother from the hood.

"Hello?" I said, raising my hand. "I'm here too."

"Hey, sis." He gave me a peck on the cheek. "Let's go to my office."

"Damn," Jackson said the instant we stepped inside Winston's huge corner office. We had a bird's-eye view of the UCLA campus as well as the jam-packed 405 freeway. Jackson made a beeline for a bronze sculpture sitting on a five-foot base. "That piece is fire."

"Tru dat," Winston said, glowing with pride. "It's a Simone Leigh creation. You should check her out."

"I will."

"I commissioned that piece," Winston said. "Nice to know you appreciate great art too."

Jackson leaned closer, examining the sculpture with admiration laced with a big dose of envy. He looked over his shoulder at me. "I don't know what happened to your sister. She has no appreciation for true art. The importance of office aesthetics either."

"Tell me about it," Winston said with a laugh. "I guess my parents didn't bless her with that gene. You should see some of the pieces my folks have in their house. Will blow your friggin' mind." He turned to me. "Mom and Dad would love to meet him. When are you inviting him over for dinner?"

"I'm not," I said without hesitation.

"Okay, fine." He put a hand on Jackson's shoulder. "Don't worry, dude, I'll hook up a visit. My mom would really dig you. She's convinced my sister will never be tied down. If she thinks y'all are hooked up, that'll take some of the pressure off me to reproduce."

"No way you're taking him to meet them. And if you do, I'll kill both of you."

Despite my threat, Winston gave Jackson a wink, and he promptly returned a conspiratorial nod. I struggled to keep my eyes from rolling out of my head.

"Let's get down to business," I said.

Once we were all seated, I dove right in. "We're working on a new case and we need to visit a patient who's in intensive care at UCLA Medical Center. I was hoping you might have some ideas about how we might get into his room."

Jackson held up his palm. "We're not asking you to do anything illegal. We don't want to put you in that type of situation."

I glared at him. "My brother knows I'd never do that."

Winston started laughing. "I like the vibe between y'all. You two hooking up yet?"

"Nah." Jackson grinned. "Not yet."

I punched him in the shoulder. "We're business partners. Nothing more. Now, can you help us?"

"Is there a guard posted outside the guy's door?" Winston asked.

"We don't know for sure," Jackson said. "But I doubt it. He was in a car accident. The police aren't involved as far as we know."

"Okay then, it's easy peasy. Just go to the hospital during visiting hours, and sign in at the visitors' desk on the first floor and get a badge, then head up to his floor. There's a buzzer outside the ICU door. They'll ask who you're there to see, then let you in."

"Don't we have to be family to visit someone in the ICU?" I asked.

"Yeah. So what? Just tell 'em you're his daughter and son-in-law or whatever."

"Aren't they going to ask for proof?" Jackson asked.

Winston shook his head. "Nope."

"They don't check IDs?" I asked.

"You'll have to show your driver's license at the visitor's desk downstairs. But you're private investigators; you must have some fake IDs you can use. Once you get to the ICU and tell them your relationship to the patient, they'll take your word for it and buzz you in."

"Really?" Jackson mused.

Winston nodded. "I don't know what you plan to do when you get there, and I don't want to know, but be aware that an ICU nurse sits right outside the room, which has glass walls so she can see into the room. But the nurses frequently step away to check on other patients."

Jackson and I looked at each other, stunned that it could really be that simple.

"It can't be that easy," I said.

Winston shrugged. "Unfortunately, it is."

Chapter 11

JACKSON

Not only did Mackenzie's brother, Dr. Winston Cunningham, possess a discerning sense of style, his tip on how to gain access to UCLA Medical Center's Intensive Care Unit was on point. A couple of fake IDs and a fairy story about Mac being Vincent Keane's stepdaughter was all it took for us to get into the ICU.

A friendly enough RN, whose name tag read Suzanne, escorted Mackenzie and me past glass-walled patient rooms. Inside each one, some poor soul lay tethered to an ordered tangle of blinking and beeping life-sustaining technology. I couldn't decide which was more unsettling: the grim hush one experiences whenever death is near or the faintest odor of cleaning supplies mixed with despair.

"How's Vincent doing?" Mackenzie asked as we continued down a wide corridor.

"He's not my patient," the nurse explained, "but I'll see if I can find his nurse and have her stop by the room to give you an update on his condition."

The last thing we needed was for someone to walk in while we were searching Keane's briefcase, but refusing to speak to his nurse would look suspicious.

Noticing a small gold cross around Suzanne's neck, I said, "My wife and I would like some time alone with Vincent to pray, but when we're done, we'll let you know."

"Of course," she said with a slow, almost pious nod of the head. "I completely understand."

I winked at Mackenzie.

"Has anyone else come to visit?" she asked the nurse.

"No. You're the first. I was told his daughter has been contacted but she lives far away, and I guess they're not on good terms. Such a shame. Do you know her?"

Mackenzie shook her head. "Not really. I mean, we met a few times when we were kids. My mom was his third wife, so . . ."

"Well, at least you're here," the nurse said. "Family's so important. Anyway, here we are." The nurse slid open the glass door and led us inside.

The surprisingly spacious room was dimly lit and shadowy. Like the other ICU patients, Vincent Keane lay unconscious, dwarfed by a dismaying number of medical devices. His pale body was barely visible beneath bandages, casts, and traction equipment. Intubation and feeding tubes came out of his lifeless face, like something out of a sci-fi horror movie. Twenty-four hours ago, Vincent Keane was a stranger to me, yet the sight of his helpless dehumanized form momentarily made my breathing grow shallow.

I could see that Mackenzie was also impacted by Keane's condition, but with the nurse present, I thought her role of concerned stepdaughter required a little more emotion. I was about to cue her with a nudge, but there was no need. Suddenly Mackenzie gasped, brought trembling hands to her face, and said, "Oh my god . . ."

As I pulled Mackenzie into a comforting hug, the nurse smiled sympathetically. "I'll go look for his nurse," she said. "There's a call button beside the bed. Just press it if you need anything."

"We will," I said, still embracing Mackenzie. "Thank you."

The instant the nurse left the room Mackenzie whispered in my ear, "Anyone watching?"

I peered through the glass wall into an empty corridor. Fortunately for us, Vincent's room wasn't in the line of sight of the nurses' station, but I wasn't ready to let go. Mac felt great in my arms.

"We're clear," I reluctantly said a minute or so later.

We dropped character and broke the embrace.

"So far, so good," Mackenzie said.

I nodded toward our comatose host. "Tell that to him."

"Not funny."

I moved to Keane's bedside. "Think he can hear us?"

"I hope not," Mackenzie said, joining me.

For a moment we stared down at Vincent Keane in respectful silence. Finally, I whispered, "Hey, Mr. Keane. If you can hear me, wiggle a finger or something."

Mackenzie groaned. "Come on. Let's get this done."

We crossed to a small seating area and Mackenzie pulled open the closet door.

Inside, there were two items resting on the floor. A sealed plastic bag, which probably contained what remained of Vincent Keane's clothing . . . and a black briefcase.

Bingo.

Considering its sixteen-thousand-dollar price tag—something I confirmed earlier with a quick Google search—Keane's briefcase couldn't have looked more average. An unadorned black rectangle with a handle, aggressively lacking in style. The words Hermès

Paris stamped on the latches were the only clue to the briefcase's true worth. Perhaps this explained why some joker at the tow yard didn't make the pricey accessory vanish from the wrecked Bentley's inventory list.

"Let me know if you see anyone coming," Mackenzie said as she laid the briefcase down on the carpet and simultaneously thumbed the dual release buttons.

The latches didn't budge.

"Damn it," she hissed, trying the buttons again and again. "It's locked."

"Not a problem." I reached into my jacket and pulled out a small black leather zipper case. My lock-picking set. "I got this."

Mackenzie and I switched places. She played lookout, while I slipped a Slim Line rake pick into the first lock. Of the eight tools in my set, the Slim Line is the quickest and perfect for simpler mechanisms, like those found on a briefcase.

I raked the tumblers while applying steady tension. I was more than a bit surprised when the small lock didn't disengage immediately. The padlocks and entry locks that I practiced on were far more sophisticated, and I could defeat those in seconds. But this ugly briefcase was being real stubborn. Some of that sixteen grand was definitely dedicated to making it a bitch to break into.

"Come on," Mackenzie said. "What's taking you so long?"

"Shhhhh. I'm trying to concentrate."

"Concentrate faster."

I quickly switched tools, replacing the Slim Line pick with the more versatile half-diamond pick. The half-diamond required more finesse, but if handled correctly it could damn near open anything.

I raked the half-diamond back and forth, ever so gently, while again applying tension. I could feel the springy resistance of each tiny tumbler, and also feel the cylinder beginning to slip. Then with a *click* the first latch sprang open.

"Yes!" I exclaimed in a hushed voice.

"Quit celebrating," Mackenzie said. "Do the other one. Hurry."

Now that I had the feel, the second lock was easy to defeat.

I swung open the briefcase and Mackenzie and I sighed at what we found inside.

A water bottle, a protein bar, a pair of Versace reading glasses, a travel chess set, and a shitload of used scratch-off lottery tickets.

What the hell?

Odder still, the briefcase's interior was as featureless as its exterior. Most briefcases were fitted with compartments of various sizes. Slots to organize credit cards, pens, business cards, and even a mobile phone. Instead, there was just a single expandable pocket with nothing inside.

"Damn," Mackenzie said. "That's it?"

"Looks like it."

"Check for a secret compartment."

"Are you kidding? There's not even a normal compartment."

"Just check."

I ran my hand over the briefcase's buttery-soft tan suede lining. If there were something hidden underneath, it would've been impossible to miss.

"Nothing," I said. "Looks like this is a bust."

As I snapped the briefcase shut, Mackenzie gasped, "Jackson, look!"

I glanced up and fixed on a sight that made my heart race and sent my mind reeling.

A freaking ninja warrior was walking down the hallway, headed toward Vincent Keane's room.

Of course, I knew I wasn't gaping at an actual ancient Japanese secret agent, but, garbed in all black, including leather gloves and a balaclava mask, this dude sure looked like one. And as Mackenzie and I watched him reach for the glass door, I knew one thing for sure, he wasn't here to deliver flowers.

Chapter 12

Get in, quick," Jackson whispered, tugging me into the closet. He eased the door shut, leaving it cracked open just enough. Our bodies were pressed so closely together that I could feel his breath on my cheek. As we peeked out and watched the masked man enter Vincent's room, several thoughts screamed for answers. Who was this person? How did he get in here? And most chilling . . . where were all the nurses and doctors?

The masked man moved to Keane's bedside, and for a moment just stared at the comatose man.

"What's he doing?" I whispered.

"Nothing good," Jackson whispered back.

He was right.

Moving with cold indifference, the masked man snatched a pillow from beneath Keane's head and jammed it down over Keane's face.

"He's trying to kill him," I said.

Jackson and I exploded from the closet.

The masked man whirled around in time to duck the sixteen-thousand-dollar briefcase Jackson hurled at his head. Missing his target, the briefcase struck the glass wall instead, turning it into a spiderweb of cracks.

I lunged forward, throwing a flurry of Krav Maga strikes.

The masked man blocked and evaded my attempted blows with scary ease, then unleashed a kick that sent me sprawling to the floor.

Jackson's turn.

He fired lefts and rights, but the masked man was crazy agile, ducking and weaving and blocking with trained efficiency. His heel shot out and the next thing I knew, Jackson was on his ass beside me on the floor.

The man not only looked like a ninja, but fought like one too.

Jackson and I jumped to our feet and pulled our guns.

The masked man grabbed hold of a rack of life-support equipment and gave it a shove.

As Jackson and I rushed forward and caught the toppling rack, the masked man took the opportunity to sprint out of the room.

Medical alarms blaring, we righted the rack then raced down the corridor in pursuit.

But the masked man was gone.

So was the entire ICU staff. Not a doctor or nurse in sight. Even the nurses' station was left unattended.

Jackson and I put away our guns and just stood there gaping at the eerily vacant unit.

"Hello?" Jackson called out.

He was immediately answered by banging and shouting. "Help! We're in here!"

We rushed toward the muffled cries for help, which appeared to be coming from a door near the end of the hallway. We could see a chair wedged underneath the doorknob.

Jackson kicked the chair out of the way and snatched the door open. Six people, a mix of doctors and nurses, sprang from a tiny medical supply closet. Their faces were stricken with panic, some of them were in tears.

"Are you okay?" I asked. But all of them shrank away from me, as if I were the threat.

Suddenly, the double doors leading into the unit burst open and a horde of police officers charged down the hallway, their guns drawn and pointed in front of them.

"Up against the wall," one of the officers yelled. "Everybody put your hands where we can see 'em. And I want everybody quiet until we figure out what's going on here."

The nurses were loudly sobbing now, as several officers ran through the unit checking each of the rooms.

"We didn't do anything wrong," Jackson said, his hands raised. "The guy you want just—"

"I said everybody quiet!" the officer shouted, nervously pointing his .38 at us.

"If you just listen," Jackson said, "I can—"

"Cuff him," the officer yelled. "Her too."

Before we could protest, two officers swung us around, slapped plastic handcuffs on our wrists, and pushed us face-first against the wall.

"Hey! Hold up," Jackson shouted. "You got it all wrong. And these cuffs are way too tight."

"We were just visiting a patient," I tried to explain. "And this guy wearing a mask walked in and tried to smother him."

"You can tell your side of the story when we get down to the station," the officer said.

"This is bullshit," Jackson said. "Talk to the nurse, she'll tell you." He spotted the nurse who'd escorted us into Keane's room a few feet away and yelled out to her. "Hey, tell them we didn't do anything wrong. We just saved that man's life."

The nurse, who was wailing and shaking, didn't even look Jackson's way.

"Give it up," I said to Jackson. "They'll take us down to the station to give a statement and then let us go."

"I'm not going anywhere."

"Just calm down. You're only making it worse."

The ICU was a madhouse now, with cops scouring the place and the rest of the staff suddenly appearing from underneath the desks at the nurses' station and from inside patients' rooms where they had been hiding during the commotion.

Jackson kept looking past me toward the nurse.

"Forget about her," I said. "She's too distraught to even talk."

"Damn," Jackson said. "I don't believe this."

When I followed his gaze, I didn't believe it either.

Lieutenant Gooden was stalking toward us with rage in his eyes. "What the hell are you guys doing here?"

"Let me explain," I said. "These cops have it all wrong. We just saved a man's life."

"What man?"

"Vincent Keane.

"And who is Vincent Keane?"

I paused a smidgen too long.

"Can I assume your interest in Keane has something to do with those three crime bosses you guys met with today?"

"You can assume anything you want," Jackson said.

"Nobody's talking to you," the lieutenant snapped.

Lieutenant Gooden waved over one of the officers and barked, "Take those cuffs off her." Then he softened his tone. "Are you okay?"

"I'm fine," I said, rubbing my wrists.

"What about me?" Jackson asked.

Lieutenant Gooden acted as if he hadn't heard him.

"Tell me what you're doing here," he asked me again.

"These cuffs are cutting off my blood supply," Jackson complained. "Can you please take them off?"

"In a minute," Lieutenant Gooden said.

Jackson glared at the lieutenant.

"C'mon," I said, "can you get someone to take his off too?"

"Not until he stops whining."

"Nobody's whining," Jackson bellowed. "This bullshit is a violation of my constitutional rights."

"Just keep mouthing off," Lieutenant Gooden fired back. "I'll show you a real violation of your constitutional rights."

Before Jackson could fully blow, I placed my hand on the lieutenant's forearm. "Mark, would you do it for me? Please."

Jackson looked as if he wanted to barf, but wisely kept his mouth shut.

Lieutenant Gooden grumbled, then instructed a cop to remove Jackson's cuffs. I struggled to stifle a laugh.

"I don't know what you think is so damn funny," Jackson said, repeatedly flexing his fingers.

I turned back to the lieutenant to keep from cracking up. "I'm sorry, Mark, but we can't tell you why we're here."

"And since we're not under arrest," Jackson added, "we're leaving."

"I have some advice for you," Lieutenant Gooden said to me. "Don't let this guy lead you down the wrong path. You're dealing with some really dangerous dudes, Mackenzie."

"Mark? Mackenzie? Oh, so y'all are on a first-name basis now?"

"Please, Mackenzie." The lieutenant gently squeezed my shoulder. "Talk to me. I can help."

"Like I said," Jackson interrupted. "I'm leaving and she's coming with me."

"We'll need a statement from both of you," Lieutenant Gooden said.

"You can call our office to schedule a time. We're out of here," Jackson said, then stalked down the hallway.

Chapter 13

JACKSON

My Mercedes was parked in an underground garage directly across the street from the hospital.

Mackenzie and I exited the hospital's main entrance, weaved through the cluster of haphazardly parked police cruisers idling out front, and headed for my car.

Once we were clear of the commotion, I said to Mackenzie, "I'll bet you a nickel that the asshole who tossed Keane's house and the asshole who tossed us is the very same asshole."

"I think you're right," she said. "I don't believe in coincidences."

"You don't believe in coincidences? What does that even mean?"

"Please don't start."

We entered the parking structure and boarded the elevator.

"If we're right," I said, "that means the masked asshole wants Keane's files to reach the DA. Either by delivering the goods himself, or by killing Keane and setting Keane's fail-safe plan in motion."

"Which means," Mackenzie said, "masked asshole has it in for Big Ced and his cronies."

"Exactly," I said. "More than likely a rival organization."

Mackenzie nodded. "I concur."

"Ooh, look at you. In a hospital for ten minutes and suddenly you *concur*."

Mackenzie chuckled. "Shut up."

The elevator dinged and we started across the parking structure in search of my car.

"This is major," I said. "Before this investigation goes any further we need to talk to Prentice. Do you *concur* with that?"

"I do," Mackenzie said. "I'll try him again." She pulled out her phone, took one look at the screen, and made a face. "No signal down here."

"Not a problem. There's the car."

I chirped the alarm. As Mackenzie and I climbed in I rubbed my aching wrists.

Mackenzie said, "Lieutenant Gooden really had you hog-tied, huh?"

"You think it's funny?"

"Just a bit."

"Well, I think it's funny how you and *Mark* are suddenly so friendly."

Mackenzie raised an eyebrow. "Jackson Jones, you sound jealous."

"Jealous? Me? Of him?"

She was right, of course. Damn straight, I was jealous.

For the sake of our partnership Mackenzie and I vowed never to become romantically entangled. Mackenzie Cunningham had it all. The super deluxe package. Beautiful, intelligent, funny, sexy. Sometimes it was pure torture working with her. At least once a day I'd find myself distracted by one of her sassy smiles. Judging from the brief but heated necking session Mac and I shared in the midst of our prior case, I could tell that she was attracted to me as well. So, yeah, the idea of Lieutenant Good-looks drooling all over my partner did rub me the wrong way. And far worse, if Mackenzie actually fell for his weak-ass game.

As if Mackenzie had a Bluetooth link to my mind, she said, "Admit it. You're feeling a little something. It's okay. I know I'm irresistible."

There was no way in hell I'd ever let her know my true feelings, so I just laughed it off and said, "Clearly you have *irresistible* confused with *irritating*." Then I hit the ignition just in time to drown out Mackenzie's undoubtedly snarky reply with the roar of my car's turbo V8.

Less than a minute later I turned out of the garage onto the street. I immediately pulled to the curb so that Mackenzie could try, once again, to reach Prentice.

She pulled out her phone and was about to hit redial when my phone chimed over the car's speaker system. *Unknown Caller* appeared on the Mercedes's central display, but Mackenzie and I somehow knew that our underworld client would be on the line.

"I see you've been trying to reach me?" Prentice's voice filled the car. "Good news, I hope?"

"Not really," I replied. "But a lot has happened that you need to know. We just left—"

"Not over the phone," Prentice interrupted. "There's a lounge on Slauson. The Come Up. Meet me there in thirty."

The call went dead.

I turned to Mackenzie. "The Come Up? Hey, isn't that your and Mark's favorite spot?"

"How'd you know?" she shot back. "You spying on us? Typical jealous behavior."

"Definitely irritating."

The Come Up was located on a quiet corner surrounded by three of the wealthiest Black neighborhoods in the state: View Park, Baldwin Hills, and Ladera Heights.

Back in the day, this area went by the nickname of the Black Beverly Hills, because of the long list of famous African American athletes, musicians, and actors who'd called the Westside enclave home.

After parking in a small adjacent lot, Mackenzie and I made our way to the entrance.

A long but narrow canopy covered a brick-lined walkway leading into the club. The bouncer/greeter, a big brother draped in a black overcoat, offered a smile and a grumbled welcome as he held the door open for us.

When we stepped inside, we were greeted by darkness highlighted by blue neon lights. A bar stretched across one section of the spacious lounge, adjacent to a small stage that was empty. Blues blasted from the speaker system, setting a laid-back mood. The place had a homey feel, like the neighborhood *Cheers* bar.

The small, mostly Black crowd was chill, a bit older than I expected, and quite beautiful. There was an ease about them that comes from winning in life. If these people didn't have it all, they sure as hell looked like it.

Prentice, rocking a purple blazer, was seated at a roped-off booth, sipping scotch and chatting with a ridiculously beautiful woman. If she wasn't a swimsuit model, she'd missed her calling.

The instant Prentice spotted us he sent the model on her way and beckoned us over.

"Welcome," he said, remaining in his seat. "Please sit."

As Mackenzie and I slid side by side into the booth, Prentice waved his hand and almost instantly a young waitress in a very short skirt appeared.

"Yes, Mr. Willis?"

"Get my guests whatever they want."

The waitress pivoted to Mackenzie and me. "Hi. What would you like?"

Mackenzie ordered white wine, of course, and I ordered whatever Prentice was drinking. It looked like scotch, and considering who he was, I knew it would be top shelf.

After receiving an approving nod from Prentice, the waitress departed to fill our orders. Then Prentice turned to me. "Excellent choice."

"Thanks. What did I order exactly?"

Prentice laughed. "Macallan 50. My private stash actually."

I didn't know much about scotch, but I did know that a bottle of fifty-year-old Macallan cost about as much as a small automobile.

"Wow," I said. "That's very generous of you. You must come here a lot."

"Of course he does," Mackenzie said, jumping in. "Willis Worldwide owns lots of bars and restaurants." She turned to Prentice. "I'm guessing this is one of them, right?"

"Close," Prentice said, wearing a small smile. "Actually, this place belongs to me and me alone. No connection to my father whatsoever, although he did try to buy me out twice. You could say the Come Up is a little side project of mine. One that I'm particularly proud of. What do you think of the place?"

"It's gorgeous," Mackenzie said. "Nice vibe."

"Really nice," I said. "Once we're done with this Keane business, I might even drop in every now and then."

"Please do," Prentice said.

The truth was I had no intention of coming back to this glitzy gangster's paradise, but I knew he'd like hearing it.

The drinks arrived.

We all clicked glasses, then Prentice watched me sip the scotch, waiting for a review.

No bullshit needed this time, the fifty-year-old Macallan was the smoothest drink that ever warmed my insides. My entire review was just a single word. *Damn!*

Pleased with that, Prentice settled back and interlocked his fingers, shifting into business mode. "Okay, tell me. Where are we?"

Mackenzie and I quickly filled Prentice in. We told him about Keane's trashed house, about the attack at the hospital, and how we believed the masked man was behind it all.

"Whoever this guy is," I said, "he's determined to get Keane's information into the DA's hands."

"In other words," Mackenzie said, "he wants to put your father, Meza, and Bioff out of business."

Prentice's reaction to this news left Mackenzie and me puzzled. He simply nodded and said, "I believe you're right."

"You don't seem very surprised." I said.

"The only thing that surprises me," Prentice said, "is that this has happened so fast. When you're on top, enemies are everywhere. And I do mean everywhere. Tell me more about this masked man."

"He's about six feet tall," I said. "Athletically built and fast as hell."

"Yeah," Mackenzie said. "He's definitely a trained fighter."

"Oh yeah," I said. "He's also white."

Prentice's brow furrowed. "Hold on. I thought you said he wore a mask."

"He did," I replied. "A black balaclava-style mask. The opening around the eyes was big enough to see some skin. White dude for sure."

Prentice stroked his beard, considering this tidbit. Finally, he said, "Could he also be Mexican?"

Mackenzie and I traded looks, instantly picking up on Prentice's suspicion.

I said to Prentice, "You really think the masked man might work for Meza or Bioff?"

"Why not? It does appear that this individual is privy to inside info. Like I said, they're everywhere. Enemies lying in wait for the perfect opportunity to replace you. This Keane mess is that opportunity . . . and some." With that he took a sip of his drink.

Mackenzie and I did the same.

"I'll look into our rat problem," Prentice finally said. "Meanwhile, you two keep going. And step it up. The masked man isn't our only problem. I've crossed paths with Lieutenant Gooden in the past. He's a pain in the ass because he's good at his job. Now that Vincent Keane is on Gooden's radar, he'll dig for a connection."

"On the plus side," Mackenzie said, "because of the murder attempt, Gooden will put a twenty-four-hour watch on Keane. Meaning the masked man won't be able to make a second attempt."

Prentice nodded. "True. But he's still out there searching for Keane's stash. You two must find it first." He glanced at his gold Rolex. "It's late. Get some sleep and get right back on this first thing. Failure is not an option. Got it?"

Mackenzie and I nodded stiffly, like two people agreeing to their own death sentences.

Chapter 14

MACKENZIE

The abrupt ringing of my cell phone jolted me from a peaceful slumber.

Groggily, I fumbled for it on the nightstand, surprised to see my brother's name scrolling across the screen. Winston was usually prepping for surgery at this time of the morning.

Before I could even say hello, his panicked voice rushed through the phone line.

"Are you okay? We've been going nuts."

His concern worried me. My brother was Mr. Chill with a capital C. Panic wasn't in his DNA.

"I'm fine," I said, rubbing my eyes and trying to get my mental bearings. "Why wouldn't I be?"

"Everybody's talking about all the chaos in the ICU yesterday? The same ICU you asked me about sneaking into. Somebody actually tried to kill a patient. Please tell me that wasn't you and your new partner."

"No, big brother, Jackson and I definitely did not try to kill a patient," I reassured him.

"So, were you there? Did you have anything to do with this?" he pressed, his voice still tinged with worry. "I can't have this coming down on me."

"Just calm down. Nothing's coming down on you."

"So what happened?" His tone turned demanding.

I wished I could confide in Winston about my new case with Big Ced, but I couldn't risk him having any knowledge that could put him in danger.

"We'd just gotten there when all the commotion started," I lied.

"Do you know the guy they were trying to kill? Is he the same guy you wanted to talk to?"

"No," I said after a long beat.

I hated lying to Winston, even though I was doing it to protect him. He was my brother and was always ready to stand by me. But I couldn't say a word to him about the dangerous mess Jackson and I were now in.

"You know I'm down with everything you do, but there's a limit. Tell me what's going on. You can trust me."

"I can't say any more. And please tell me Mom doesn't know about all this."

"Of course she knows. It was all over the news. She called me in a panic to make sure I was okay."

My heart leaped into my throat. "You told Mom about Jackson and me wanting to get into the ICU?"

"Of course I didn't tell her that."

My pulse slowly retreated to a normal range. "Thanks for not saying anything."

"You're welcome. But you know you can trust me. Tell me what's really going on. If this is going to be like your last case, where you and Jackson were running all over town with people trying to kill you, I need to know that."

There was a long pause in the conversation. Winston waited me out.

"I know I can trust you," I finally said, "but don't worry, I'll be fine."

"You better be," Winston said. "Or Jackson Jones is going to have to answer to me."

"I'm an adult and a damn good private investigator. I can take care of myself."

"So you say. Sis, you don't always have to be Superwoman. Please be careful."

Hanging up the phone, I rolled onto my back and stared up at the ceiling.

I was in no mood to be embroiled in another case that had a bull's-eye on my back. And I prayed that whatever madness Jackson and I had gotten ourselves into wasn't going to end up with us running for our lives yet again.

Chapter 15

JACKSON

It was a cloudless night.

The moon enormous.

I stood in an empty parking lot, surrounded by four ninja warriors, each wielding a moonlight-kissed samurai sword. Four pairs of murderous eyes glared at me from behind black balaclava masks.

My trembling hands were empty.

My heart hammered.

My eyes darted, seeking a way to escape.

The four ninjas unleashed bloodthirsty screams and charged toward me.

I clenched my eyes shut, ready to be sliced to shreds, but . . .

A telephone rang.

My attackers froze in their tracks, lowered their swords, and just watched as I reached into my jacket and pulled out my ringing cell phone.

And that's when I woke up.

My iPhone was screaming for attention on my bedside table.

As I winced at the morning sunlight stabbing through my blinds, the persistent barking dog ringtone told me that the incoming call was from my ex-wife, Robin. While it was possible Nicole was using her mom's phone to call me, as my baby girl often did, the too-early-in-the-morning wake-up call was a Robin classic. According to her, she got up every day at 6 a.m. and so that's when everyone else's day started too.

It still baffles me that I was married to this woman. She's gorgeous as hell, which was why I missed all the warning signs that she might not be wifey material.

I didn't know why Robin was calling me, but before I could deal with her I needed a shower and a strong cup of coffee.

I let the call go to voicemail, knowing that if it was truly important, she'd just call back.

As I rolled out of bed I winced at a dull pain in my midsection, courtesy of the masked man's perfectly placed straight kick. That dude nailed me so hard that I was having nightmares about him. Whoever he was, he really knew how to handle himself. Even Mackenzie, with all her fancy kung fu moves, couldn't touch the guy.

I wondered if Mackenzie also had a nightmare about the masked man. Nah. All her dream time was probably taken up with visions of Lieutenant Good-stuff.

The shower felt so good that I remained under the rainfall showerhead for an extra five minutes, lost in relaxing thoughts. Like, after the Keane business was done, I'd finally be able to upgrade my ride. Maybe it was time to go electric.

As I stood in my kitchen, garbed in a terry cloth robe, waiting for my espresso to brew, my cell phone rang again. I winced, assuming Robin was taking a second stab at ruining my morning by calling me from a different phone, but I was relieved to see the name *Roxanna* on my iPhone's screen.

"Hey, Roxy. What's up?"

"This you tell me," Roxanna shot back in Czech-accented English. "The hospital is all over the news. I want to make sure you and Mackenzie are okay."

"There was a little tussle," I said, "but we're fine."

"Why you not call me?" she said, her tone still sharp. "I worry about you. I'm Roma. You know this, yes? Sometimes I get very scary feelings inside."

When I first met Roxanna, she shared with me her Czech Romani heritage, explaining that for her people, being labeled "Gypsy" carried the same offensive weight as the N-word does for African Americans.

Believe me, I never forgot that.

I said to her, "Roxy, I'm sorry. You're right. I should've called you."

"Please remember next time," she said, her voice calmer now. "Anyway, I'm just glad you are not hurt, *má laská.*"

"You said the story was all over the news? Is that true?"

"Turn on TV. KTLA."

"Hold on." I grabbed my espresso, moved into the living room, and poked my remote until the *KTLA Morning News* show filled my eighty-inch flat screen. The field reporter Gale Anderson was broadcasting live from outside the UCLA Medical Center. She delivered the juicy broad strokes—patient attacked by masked man in the ICU, staff held prisoner—but offered very few details. Apparently, Lieutenant Gooden left my and Mackenzie's names out of the official LAPD statement, because we were never mentioned. This was a good thing, because reporters tailing us night and day would definitely slow down our hunt for Keane's info stash.

I switched the channel to *Good Day L.A.* on Fox and caught the tail end of what they were calling the UCLA ICU ATTACK.

"You're right," I said into the phone. "It's everywhere."

"Who is this man in mask?" Roxanna asked.

I paused.

Mackenzie and I had agreed to tell Roxanna as little as possible in order to keep her safe. But there was no way she could do the research we needed without knowing the full story. So I told her. Everything.

"Much, much danger!" Rox said, true alarm in her voice.

"We get that," I said, "but it's too late for us to worry about that now."

I could almost see the distraught look on Roxanna's face.

"You asked about the masked man," I continued. "Well, we think he's the competition. Someone who wants Keane's information to come out and really shake shit up. Prentice thinks he's connected to an insider. Someone working for either Bioff or Meza who's decided to make a power grab."

"Jackson, *můj miláček*, this business sounds to me very dangerous. You must find way out."

"It's not that easy," I told her. "Not with these people. Our best play is to get our hands on Keane's files before that masked asshole does. Prentice said he's going to do some snake hunting, and I think there's a way you can help."

"Anything," Roxanna replied. "Tell me."

"The masked man knew how to handle himself. Do some digging into Bioff's and Meza's organizations. Look for someone with a background in boxing or martial arts. Pro level. Either this dude's possessed by Bruce Lee or he's been in the ring before."

"I check right away," Roxanna said. "Just promise me that you and Mackenzie will be careful. Please."

The heartfelt concern in Roxanna's voice shook me up. The realization hit me that Roxy wasn't merely my *man in the chair*, she was a real friend. She genuinely cared about me. Her words warmed me and put an honest-to-god lump in my throat.

I made a mental note to buy my Roma BFF something amazing once this Vincent Keane mess was all wrapped up and Safe and Sound's business account was several zeroes fatter.

"Jackson," Roxanna's voice snapped me out of my reverie, "I really need you to make me this promise. I need to hear you say these words."

"I promise," I said to Roxanna. "I promise that Mac and I will be very careful."

Roxanna sighed.

"What's wrong?"

"No. I should not say."

"Roxanna, tell me."

She sighed again, then said, "Your promise, it did not help. I still have a very terrible feeling that I will never see you and Mackenzie again."

Chapter 16

MACKENZIE

By the time I made it to the office, I was surprised to find Jackson already settled in. He was comfortably leaning back in his chair, his hands interlocked behind his head, his feet casually propped up on the desk.

"You certainly look relaxed," I said.

"Just the opposite. This is my thinking pose."

"Yeah, okay. I didn't see your car in the garage."

"It's there. Those parking stalls are way too small. I don't want anybody denting my car doors. I found a special parking spot hidden away in a back corner."

"Of course you did."

Nadine knocked on the open door and stepped inside. "Here's all the information, perfectly indexed and organized," she said, handing a folder to Jackson and another one to me. "I made a duplicate copy for you."

"What's this?" I asked.

"The information we got from our new client yesterday," Jackson said. "Plus whatever Nadine could find on the internet about the people mentioned in the file. Nadine is an absolute magician."

She smiled in agreement. "There's some interesting stuff in there. I think you should begin by—"

Jackson raised a hand, cutting her off. "That's okay. We're good."

"No," I said, placing my bag in my chair and sitting on the edge of my desk. "I'd like to hear your thoughts. Three heads are better than two, especially when two of the three are female."

"I love this woman," Nadine said, taking a seat in front of me.

Jackson frowned as he placed his feet on the floor and sat up in his chair.

"So, go on," I encouraged her. "Tell us what you think?"

Nadine's eyes actually lit up.

"After reading through all the info, there were only three people listed. Elizabeth, Vincent Keane's ex-wife. Yolonda Chin, a woman who made weekly *house calls*." Nadine paused to make air quotes with her fingers. "And Rebecca, Vincent's estranged daughter. His ex-wife—"

"Is dead," Jackson said, rudely interrupting her. "We appreciate all your work. We'll take it from here."

"I was just going to suggest that you—"

"I said we'll take it from here." Jackson's tone was unusually gruff.

Nadine's shoulders slumped. "Whatever you say, boss." As she stood up, her whole body seemed to deflate. "Let me know if you need anything else."

When she was gone, I lit into Jackson. "You were really out of line. What's the harm in listening to her thoughts?"

"My cousin is our assistant, not our junior PI."

"We could use a junior PI. She clearly gets a kick out of this work. Why not encourage her?"

"Maybe at some point down the line we can bring her in on a case, but not this one."

"Why not?" I pushed. "We could use the help."

"Are you kidding me? We're dealing with some really danger-ous dudes here. I didn't tell Nadine anything about Big Ced or the other guys. Only that we're trying to find people who knew Vin-cent. The less she knows about the real deal, the better."

"I just don't understand why you dismissed her like that."

"Because I care about her," Jackson snapped. "That's why. It's one thing for us to be putting ourselves at risk working for these guys. But if the tables turn like they did in our last case and some-body comes after us, I don't want my cousin anywhere near the drama. I hated even telling Roxy the real deal, but I had no choice."

I couldn't argue with that. I actually admired Jackson for look-ing out for Nadine. Still, I felt bad about the way he had dashed her enthusiasm. I planned to let her know that we appreciated her efforts and would definitely use her on a case in the future.

"You're absolutely right," I said, sitting down behind my desk. "I should have been on the same page."

Jackson smiled. "Wow, twice in two days. *You're absolutely right.* I can't help it. I get a little turned on hearing you say those words to me."

"You do realize that I'm never going to say them again, right?"

He grinned. "Let's just go through the file and figure out our next move."

I opened the folder and began studying the information inside as Jackson did the same. The additional stuff Nadine had pulled from the internet was impressive. It included general background infor-mation on each of the three people, their most recent addresses, and their social media profiles.

Twenty minutes later, Jackson looked across the room at me.

"You done yet?"

"Nope. Still reading."

"Well, hurry up."

"Just give me a minute."

"Interesting," he said. "You're the one with the Ivy League college degree, and yet . . ."

"Could you please just shut up?"

Jackson propped up his feet on his desk again and folded his arms across his chest. He started whistling, but abruptly stopped when I glared at him.

About ten minutes later, I was done.

"I wonder if Vincent had a will," I said. "That would be one place to leave the instructions. Did you ask Nadine to find out if he had a lawyer?"

Jackson nodded. "Yep. And she found no evidence that he did. I doubt a guy in his line of work would've even trusted a lawyer with this kind of stuff. But if he did put it in a will, he probably drafted it himself since he was a lawyer."

"Assuming there is a will," I said, "whoever trashed his house obviously didn't find it or they wouldn't have come for him in the hospital."

Jackson shrugged. "Leaving it in a will is too simple. My gut says he gave the info to someone he trusted."

"Okay," I said, "the ex-wife is off the table since she's no longer around. That leaves his paid lover and his daughter. Let's talk to them."

Jackson nodded as he began flipping through the file again.

"I think we should start with Yolonda Chin. He probably trusted her more than his daughter. He's been hooking up with her for a long time. I'd bet good money that they've shared a lot of pillow talk."

"You're thinking like a man. We should start with the daughter. It could be a good thing that they're on the outs. If she has a grudge against her father, she might be more willing to tell all. Even if she knows nothing about his file, she could lead us to someone who does."

"We'll get to her," Jackson said, "but I think we should start with Chin for one very important reason."

"And what's that?"

"She lives thirty minutes away in Monterey Park. That's a helluva lot closer than the two-hour drive to the daughter's place in Bakersfield."

Chapter 17

JACKSON

Traffic on the 10 freeway was less of a log jam than normal so the drive to Monterey Park took only twenty-five minutes. Located eight miles east of Downtown Los Angeles, the upscale Asian American community was SoCal famous for its authentic Chinese restaurants. I've heard Monterey Park described as a suburban Chinatown, but as we cruised along a busy avenue, I saw very little to justify that nickname. Sure, there were a few shop signs that I couldn't read, but, just like everywhere else in America, fast-food chains, big-box stores, and supermarkets seemed to go on forever.

"You ever been out this way before?" I asked Mackenzie.

She shook her head. "No. At least I don't think so."

"The Chinese restaurants are supposed to be amazing. Let's grab some lunch after we're done."

She made a face. "I'm not a big fan of Chinese food."

I laughed. "You're kidding, right?"

Mackenzie groaned. "All my life I get that same reaction. Not everyone likes Chinese food, you know."

"Oh yeah. Name three."

Mackenzie smacked her lips. "You're so annoying sometimes."

"You're weird all the time."

If you typed "middle-class suburb" into Google, you'd get dozens of photos that looked exactly like Yolonda's block. Unremarkable homes on an unremarkable street. Beautiful artificial lawns, a Tesla in every other driveway, and a Ring camera guarding every front door. The twenty-first-century version of the American dream.

Yolonda's house was smack-dab in the middle of the block and the only one with a red door. An interesting touch considering her profession. Either Ms. Chin had a devil-may-care sense of humor or she was completely clueless.

I parked directly out front and Mac and I approached the front door. Before I could press the Ring doorbell, a female voice squawked from the device. "No Jehovahs, please."

"Wait," I said. "We're not Jehovah's Witnesses. Are you Ms. Chin?"

"What do you want?"

"I'm Jackson Jones and this is my partner, Mackenzie Cunningham. We're—"

"Police?"

"No, ma'am," Mackenzie said. "We're not with the police. We're private investigators. We'd like to talk to you about Vincent Keane."

"What? You're saying Vince sent you here?"

Mackenzie sidestepped the question. "Are you aware that Mr. Keane was in a car accident?"

Over the Ring's speaker Yolonda's gasp sounded like a burst of static. "Oh no," she said. "Is he okay?"

I said, "Ms. Chin, if we could just—"

"Wait. Hold on."

An instant later the red door swung open. Yolonda Chin's face was tight with worry, but this did nothing to diminish her beauty.

Her file said she was thirty-seven but, with her long raven hair pulled back in a ponytail, she looked ten years younger. The skin-tight jumpsuit she wore clung to a slender yoga-toned physique. But what really caught my eye were Yolonda's fingernails. Pointy, glossy red with meticulously applied glittering accents. Nail art taken to the nth degree.

"Please," Yolonda said. "Don't tell me my Vince is dead."

"He's not," Mackenzie said. "But he is in a coma."

"Oh no." She cupped her mouth with her hand. "How bad is it?"

"Do you mind if we talk inside?" I said.

Yolonda's face changed. Concern turned to caution. She blatantly looked us up and down, then said, "Are you sure you're not cops?"

Mackenzie handed her a business card.

Yolonda looked it over then nodded and took a step back. "Come in."

A moment later we stood in Yolonda Chin's living room. The place was clean and thoughtfully decorated. Lots of plants and no TV. An unrolled yoga mat in the middle of the floor and the water bottle beside it told me that we had interrupted her workout. Yolonda cleared a few throw pillows from her sofa and invited us to sit, but I assured her we wouldn't be staying long.

"What do the doctors say?" she asked. "Will he wake up?"

"Honestly," I told her, "we're not sure, but his injuries are pretty severe."

"Poor, poor Vince."

Mackenzie asked, "Were you and Vincent really close?"

Yolonda shrugged. "Sure. I mean he was my best client. I give erotic massages. Vince was every Thursday afternoon. Three hours minimum. Sometimes longer. Depends on how frisky he felt."

Mackenzie and I traded a glance.

She chuckled at our reaction. "That's right. No shame in my game. I provide a much-needed service and Yoyo's the best. Vince tips very well." Then she frowned. "Now I know why he didn't call this week. I figured he was out of town or something. What hospital is he in?"

"UCLA Medical Center," Mackenzie said, "but the police are guarding him. I doubt they'd allow any visitors."

Yolonda's brow wrinkled. "Police? But why would the police—wait. That thing on the news about that man attacked in a hospital. That was Vince?"

"It was," I said. "That's kind of why we're here."

"I don't understand."

"Did Vincent leave you anything in case he died?"

The furrows on Yolonda's brow deepened. "Say that again."

"I know how this sounds," I said, "but did Vincent leave you anything that you're not supposed to open until he dies? You know, maybe a box or an envelope."

"Or maybe just instructions on what to do," Mackenzie added.

For a tense beat Yolonda regarded us with narrowed eyes. Finally, she asked, "Who hired you two?"

"That's confidential," I said. "Why? Does it matter?"

"It does matter," Yolonda said, "because Vince told me that absolutely nobody would know about the package."

"So Vincent did leave you a package," I said.

Yolonda nodded slowly. "He sure did. 'Only open after my funeral,' he said. He even made me swear on my grandmother's grave."

"Is the package here?" Mackenzie asked. "Can you show it to us?"

Yolonda wagged one of her perfect fingernails. "I don't think so. You said Vince is in a coma, not dead. Am I right?"

Mackenzie said, "Yes, but—"

"No buts." Yolonda crossed her arms. "Vince's instructions were very clear."

"Look," I said. "You're smart. You must know that Vincent isn't exactly on the up-and-up. He deals with some very shady people."

"Yeah, and?"

"Well, those shady people would do anything to get that envelope. Look at what happened to Vincent in the hospital."

Mackenzie jumped in. "It's not safe for you to have it in your possession."

After a moment's thought, Yolonda replied, "So what you're saying is . . . the contents of this envelope are valuable."

"In a way, yes," I said. "But not how you think. It doesn't contain money or anything."

"What does it contain?"

"We can't say," Mackenzie said.

"Then you can't have it," Yolonda said. "Unless—"

"Unless what?" I said.

Yolonda cocked her head, an opportunistic twinkle in her eye. "Let me ask you this. How much do you think it's worth?"

Mac and I traded smiles, charmed by Yolonda's savvy and relieved that the only thing separating us from that envelope was a little cash.

I pulled out my wallet and removed all the bills. "There's a little over five hundred here," I told Yolonda. "Will that work?"

Yolonda laughed. "Twenty thousand and it's yours. Cash money, of course."

Mackenzie and I blurted out, "What?"

"Do you think Yoyo is stupid?"

"Ms. Chin, please," I said. "We don't have twenty thousand dollars to—"

She held up a hand like a traffic cop. "Stop. Private investigators work for someone. Usually rich people. If they can afford to hire you, they can afford to pay me. Make sense? I think it does."

Actually, Yolonda *was* making sense. In fact, I was pretty sure Big Ced and his cohorts would pay a lot more than twenty grand to get their hands on Vincent's poison file. The look on Mackenzie's face told me she had reached the same conclusion. Considering what was at stake, Yolonda's demand was actually a bargain.

"All right," I said to Yolonda. "I think we can make this happen. Just give us a couple of hours."

She threw up her hands. "Sure. But remember, cash first, then you get the package. Cash must be first."

"That's fine," I said.

As we walked back to my car, Mackenzie asked, "Do you trust her?"

"Are you kidding?" I replied. "But what choice do we have? We have to play this through."

Chapter 18

MACKENZIE

An hour later, we were back in Downtown Los Angeles, lounging in the plush lobby of Willis Worldwide. Instead of being taken to the conference room, this time a receptionist led us down a lengthy corridor. She stopped at an unassuming door and punched in a code. The door clicked open and took us down another corridor and finally to a corner office. Or more like a corner suite.

Prentice was sitting behind a shiny cherrywood desk the size of a horizontal refrigerator. The office exuded opulence to the point of excess. Thick gold drapes framed a large window, offering a view of a smog-choked LA skyline. The artwork looked like it belonged in an art gallery. A mammoth TV hung along one wall, tuned to CNBC, its screen cluttered with stock market ticker symbols. Prentice obviously had a thing for gold because there was a ton of it. Gold stapler and pencil holder on his desk, gold-framed artwork on the walls, even a gold replica of the company's logo. This son of a boss was definitely overcompensating for something.

"Wow," Prentice said as he rose from his seat and rounded the desk. "You guys already have a lead?" He grinned as he extended his hand. "I guess that's why you have such a stellar reputation."

He was impeccably dressed in his trademark designer suit, accessorized with a glistening diamond wedding band that I hadn't noticed before, though I couldn't fathom how I had missed it. I'm sure my partner was smitten.

As we took seats next to each other on a white leather sofa tucked in the corner of the room, Jackson whispered out of the side of his mouth, "Now, this is how you decorate an office."

I shook my head and whispered back. "Yeah, if your ego requires a palace to fit it."

"I really like your office decor," Jackson said, as our new client sat down across from us on a matching sofa. "The drapes are a nice touch. We're in the middle of decorating our new office. You have to share the name of your interior decorator."

My expression must have conveyed my mindset, because Prentice chuckled. "I'd be glad to, but I'm not sure your partner shares the same sentiment."

"I'm sorry," I said. "It's not exactly my style."

"My father feels the same way, but he's old school. A desk and a couple of chairs, and he's good to go. I tease him that his bland office looks like a barn. Convincing him to let my designer decorate the lobby and conference room took some doing."

"That lobby is on point," Jackson said, apparently for my benefit. "An office space should communicate who you are and what you stand for."

"Exactly," Prentice said, punching the air with his finger to emphasize the point. "You have to exude power to attract power."

If Jackson thought our office was going to look anything like this he was kidding himself. "To each his own," I said.

"Fair enough." Prentice eagerly rubbed his palms together. "So let's get down to business. I hope you're here because you have some good news for me."

"We do," Jackson began cautiously, "but it comes with a catch."

Jackson briefed Prentice on our visit to Yolonda's place, telling him about the package Vincent had entrusted to her, stipulating that she should only open it after his death.

Prentice leaned back and stretched his arm along the back of the couch. "So where is it? Do you guys have it?"

"Not yet," Jackson said, briefly inhaling. "She'll give it up, but only in exchange for twenty grand."

Prentice stroked his chin but didn't say anything. We patiently waited for him to speak. More specifically, for him to say that he was going to give us the twenty grand Yolonda was demanding.

"You think she's on the up-and-up?" he finally asked. "That she really has the evidence?"

Jackson was about to respond, but I cut him off, fearing he might overpromise. "We think so, but we can't know for sure until we see it. They've had an arrangement for years. She seems to be the closest person to him and the one he'd most likely trust with that kind of sensitive information."

Prentice nodded several times. "Let me consult with my father and the others. I'll need their approval."

"Understood," Jackson said, getting to his feet. "How long do you think that'll take?"

"Give me a couple of hours."

• • •

We received a call about an hour later giving us the go-ahead. Jackson and I were now on our way back to Monterey Park, carrying a large envelope stuffed with crisp one-hundred-dollar bills.

"You think they keep a stash of cash in the office?" Jackson asked me.

"If not there, then someplace close, because he sure came up with the money fast."

"We're working pretty fast, too," he said. "I can't believe we've already wrapped up this case."

"You're getting ahead of yourself. You haven't seen what's in that package yet."

Jackson frowned. "Stop raining on my parade. Sometimes things just fall into place. What else could be in it except the evidence?"

Maybe he was right, but I wouldn't be saying that out loud again. Perhaps this was an omen that teaming up with Jackson was a wise decision. Not only were we about to resolve our first case, we were also earning the biggest payout of our careers. Nadine had already deposited the fifty-grand check and now we'd have another one hundred and fifty thousand dollars to add to our joint bank account. Not a bad start.

"I guess it wouldn't hurt to splurge a little on office decor," I said.

Jackson smiled from ear to ear. "I love the sound of that."

"Don't get carried away. I said splurge *a little*."

"I wonder how much Prentice's decorator charges."

"Wonder all you want. We most definitely are *not* hiring her."

Jackson frowned. "Let's just request a consultation; it'll probably be free. We might be able to steal a few good ideas from her."

"No way. We can come up with our own ideas. Taj Mahal chic isn't exactly the look we should be going for. So forget it."

Chapter 19

JACKSON

Yolonda Chin's Ring doorbell had been smashed to hell. The black rectangular device dangled from its mount by a single frayed wire, and the lens was shattered.

Mackenzie and I stood on the walk, about three steps from the front door, staring at the damage, both of us frozen by the near certainty that something was now very wrong behind that big red door.

"Shit!"

Mackenzie and I drew our handguns and rushed forward. The front door was unlocked. Another bad sign.

As we charged inside Mackenzie called out, "Miss Chin, are you all right!"

The living room was empty but there were signs of a struggle. The coffee table overturned, toppled plants, and an iPhone on the floor . . . beside a broken red fingernail.

"Miss Chin," I shouted. "Are you here? Hello?"

A feeble voice replied from the direction of the bedrooms. "Help."

Mackenzie and I sprinted down a short hall. The first bedroom was empty. We hurried to the end of the hall and into what appeared to be the master bedroom.

That's where we found her.

Yolonda Chin was spread-eagled on the bed, her wrists and ankles lashed to the bedposts. Her pink jumpsuit was now marred with what looked like crimson polka dots.

The fact that Yolonda was still alive was a miracle.

"Help me," she sobbed. "Please."

"Call an ambulance," I said to Mackenzie. "But don't use your phone. Use the house phone. It's in the living room."

As Mackenzie raced to retrieve the phone, I began to free Yolonda's wrists. They were bound so tight that her hands had turned blue.

Even though I was pretty sure I knew the answer, I asked the question anyway. "What happened?"

She strained to get words out through sobs. "A . . . a man. In a mask. He . . . he wanted the package too. I told him I lied. That . . . that I didn't have it. Vince never gave me anything. But he . . . he didn't believe me, and—"

Yolonda winced and gasped, then her eyes dulled and her face went slack.

"Yolonda!"

Her eyes closed and Yolonda Chin was gone.

Mackenzie burst back into the bedroom clutching the receiver of Yolonda's house phone. "What's the address?"

"Forget it," I said. "She's dead."

"Oh god, no." Mackenzie dropped Yolonda's phone and backed up against the wall.

"It was him," I said. "The guy in the mask."

"How do you know that?"

"She told me. She also said she lied about the package. Point is, that masked bastard had the same bogus information we had, which proves—"

Mackenzie pointed. "What's that? There's something in her hand."

A slip of white paper was clutched in Yolonda's right hand. I peeled open her death grip and removed the paper. The fact that it was folded just so caused a chill to ripple through me.

"It's from him," Mackenzie murmured.

"Yeah."

Slowly, I unfolded it. The two words scrawled on that paper sent my pulse into overdrive.

Tick tock!

I yelled at Mackenzie. "Get out of here now!"

We ran back through the house, knocking over anything in our path, and practically leaped out the front door. Just in time too.

KAFUCKINGBOOM!

Yolonda's unremarkable ranch-style house blew up quite spectacularly.

The pressure wave blasted me and Mackenzie to our asses on the front lawn as Yolonda's big red door flew off its hinges and into the air in what looked like slow-motion flight. I grabbed Mackenzie by the arm, pulling her on top of me.

"What are you doing?"

Ignoring her question, I wrapped my arms firmly around her and hurled us both sideways. We tumbled several yards away as the door landed in the exact spot where we'd been lying.

"You saved my life," Mackenzie gasped, collapsing against my chest, her head buried in the crook of my neck.

"I saved both of our lives," I said, squeezing her even tighter.

As what remained of Yolonda's house went up in flames, Mackenzie, still panting, said aloud exactly what I was thinking: "That was meant for us."

Chapter 20

MACKENZIE

Jackson and I hightailed it to his car, jumped inside, and sped down the street. For the first few minutes of our drive, we were both too rattled to speak. The only sound was our labored breathing.

The images of Yolanda's home engulfed in towering flames and that door hurtling toward us replayed in my mind. I suspected Jackson was grappling with the same.

Just hours ago, we were excited about having some extra cash to spruce up our new office. Now we were both shook up. Had it taken us a few seconds longer to notice the piece of paper in Yolanda's hand, we'd both be dead.

I finally broke the silence. "I don't think Big Ced, Bioff, and Meza are the united front they appear to be."

Jackson took his eyes from the road to look at me. "You're reading my mind. It's no coincidence that minutes after we tell Prentice about Chin, somebody kills her. He must have told his father and his two cronies."

"The guy in the mask is probably working for one of the three crime bosses," I said.

"Yep," Jackson said. "But which one?"

He reached for his phone and called Roxanna, placing the call on speaker.

"Were you able to find anything?" he asked.

"No, *moje láska*. No info on man in mask. He is big mystery."

"Anyone turn up with a professional fighting background?"

"No can find that information," Roxanna said.

"What about skills with explosives?" I asked.

"I must check. Get back to you."

Jackson told Roxanna about the explosion at Chin's house and our narrow escape.

"I need you to access Chin's home security system and download all video from today, then erase it from the system and the cloud. I don't want the police to know we were there."

"Understood," Roxanna said. "But that's not enough. I erase all cameras in neighborhood. I take whole systems down for blocks. You two would be on those cameras too."

"You're the best," Jackson said.

"Okay, *moje láska*. You two be safe."

"We will," Jackson told her. "Right now we have some important business to take care of."

"I hope that important business is telling Prentice we're done with this case," I said, after he hung up.

"It is," Jackson said. "Prentice's office is exactly where we're headed now."

I relished being a private investigator, finding it thrilling to decipher what I liked to call people puzzles. I didn't, however, have a superhero complex and I wanted nothing to do with the dangerous criminals we were now mixed up with. No amount of money was worth putting our lives on the line. Again.

"But what if Big Ced refuses to let us out?" I asked.

Jackson went quiet for a long stretch before responding. "Then we'll have to call your boyfriend, Lieutenant Goodie."

The fact that Jackson would be willing to turn to the lieutenant for help was an indication of just how much danger we were in.

Twenty minutes later, we arrived at Willis Worldwide. The receptionist escorted us into Prentice's office, only to find it empty. I collapsed onto the white sofa, mentally drained, while Jackson started walking back and forth in front of the window like an agitated robot.

"Please sit down," I said. "You're making me even more nervous."

He ignored me and kept pacing.

The office door opened and before Prentice was barely inside, Jackson charged up to him. "Yolonda Chin's dead and we're lucky we're not corpses, too," Jackson yelled, his voice brimming with anger. "This is not what we signed up for."

"Calm down," Prentice told him as he made his way over to where I was sitting. "Have a seat and tell me what happened."

Jackson reluctantly sat down next to me and quickly recapped what had occurred during our return trip to Monterey Park, explaining that Yolonda had lied to us, and in the process gotten herself killed.

"Did you find out yet whether it's Bioff or Meza who's working against you?" Jackson asked.

Prentice shook his head. "No. My guys came up with nothing."

"When you got approval for the twenty grand, did you tell Bioff and Meza that we had located Chin?"

He nodded.

"Think about it. Barely an hour after you did that, the woman is murdered. How would anyone else know about her? And the killer leaves a note that basically says our time is up too. "

"Or that you had hired us," I chimed in. "Someone knew we

were headed back there and wrote that note as a direct message to us. And it makes the most sense that it's one of them."

Prentice grew still, then slowly nodded as the realization set in. "Those muthafuckers."

"It's irrelevant to us whether the guy is working for Bioff or Meza, or both of them," Jackson said. "This job is way too dangerous. We're done."

"Hold your horses," Prentice said, showing us his palms. "I'll continue to look into this. I'll also speak to my father about upping your fee."

"No need to do that," I said. "Like Jackson said, we're out."

Prentice leaned back on the couch and casually extended both arms along the back. "If it were up to me, I'd let you walk. But my father and his cohorts won't. So quitting the case is not an option."

I sucked in a big breath and didn't let it out.

"Your only way off this case is to find the evidence."

"And if we refuse?" Jackson boldly asked.

Prentice's lips curled into a menacing smile. "Do you really need me to spell it out?"

My stomach clenched with fear, and I sensed that Jackson was experiencing the same.

"Yeah," Jackson said, "spell it out."

"Okay," he said, his eyes locked on Jackson's. "One morning you'll be sitting on the Venice boardwalk, sipping a cup of coffee, laced with an untraceable drug. Three days later, you'll die of a heart attack."

Prentice turned to me. "And you," he said, pointing his index finger. "Perhaps you'll be doing one of your hill runs at Kenneth Hahn Park when two vicious pit bulls appear from nowhere and tear you to shreds. What an unfortunate accident."

I briefly shut my eyes.

"So," Prentice continued, his gaze back on Jackson. "Do you really want to spend the rest of your days looking over your shoulder?"

Jackson slumped.

"Don't look so sad," Prentice said, trying to lighten the mood. "I do have some good news for you. I just got word that Vincent is expected to pull through."

Jackson and I exchanged a puzzled glance. "Why is that good news for us?" he asked.

"Because now you have more time to do what you've been hired to do: find that evidence."

Jackson let out an audible sigh, while I quietly suppressed my exasperation.

Prentice stood up. "So I guess you two better get back to work. Time is of the essence."

Chapter 21

JACKSON

Like folks tend to do after a burial service, Mackenzie and I remained soberly quiet as we made our way back to my car.

Yesterday, when we were low-key coerced into working for Big Ced, Meza, and Bioff, Mac and I knew we were caught up in something precarious. But the gig seemed, at most, like a flirtation with danger. We brought our A-game and played it straight; the treacherous trio would twist our arms only so far. After all, we're not a part of their underworld. We're law-abiding citizens. We're just the hired help.

We couldn't have been more wrong.

I've been threatened countless times, but it's different when the threat comes from the son of the most dangerous man in Los Angeles. There was no longer any doubt. If we didn't make Big Ced happy, he'd make us dead. And to make things worse, there was also a masked maniac somewhere out there, trying to blow us up.

The instant we climbed into my Benz, Mackenzie broke the silence. "What are we going to do?"

I could hear the unease in her voice. I wanted to reach out and take her hand, not just to comfort her, but to soothe my jangled nerves as well. But I decided against it. My partner prided herself on her toughness and didn't respond well to being treated like a gentle flower. Also, curling up and cowering together was most definitely the wrong move. Fear paralyzes. What we needed now was to keep it moving and solve this damn case.

With as much confidence as I could muster, I said to Mackenzie, "We'll just keep doing what we've been doing. Chasing down every lead to get these goons what they want."

Mackenzie sighed. "Maybe we should reconsider letting Mark help us."

Hearing her evoke that guy's name, like he was some kind of white knight, made my jaw ache. "No way," I said, shaking my head. "I think there's still a chance they'd let us walk away, even if we come up empty. But going to the police is a line we can't uncross. Nothing would ever be the same for us. Sorry, but your boyfriend can't save us."

Mackenzie leveled a glare on me. "Not now. I'm not in the mood."

"Okay. Sorry." She was right. This wasn't the time to poke her . . . or for me to get distracted by a pang of jealousy.

She went on. "We keep it moving, I agree with that. But what about that man trying to kill us?"

Before I could open my mouth, she answered her own question. "Until this case is closed, I think we should stay together. Always."

"Hold up. When you say always, do you mean always?"

"Yes, you can sleep on my couch."

"Okay, I said I agree that we should watch each other's backs, night and day. But why your place and not mine?"

Mackenzie laughed. "Because I can only imagine what your man cave is like."

"Fine, but if I'm going to stay with you I gotta grab some stuff from home. So no need to imagine. You get to see it for yourself."

"Oh joy," Mackenzie said, clutching her heart with both hands. "Lucky me."

Moments later we were navigating mid-afternoon street traffic, through Downtown Los Angeles, headed for the 10 freeway. Mackenzie and I were discussing our plan to drive out to Bakersfield tomorrow to chat with Keane's daughter, when I noticed that we were being followed.

Over a span of ten minutes, I spotted the same black SUV tailing us. Even after we'd made a few turns, it was still there, always a few cars back. Lots of downtown traffic funneled toward the highway, so seeing the same vehicle could've easily been a coincidence, but my gut wasn't happy. Years of police and PI experience yelled, *fuck coincidence. That black SUV is trouble.*

"What's wrong?" Mac said, noticing my fixation on the rearview mirror.

"I think we're being followed. Black SUV. Two cars back."

Mackenzie glanced over her shoulder. "I see it. Are you sure?"

"Every turn I make, that SUV makes."

Mackenzie made a face. "Yeah, but—"

"But nothing," I said. "Considering we're on someone's hit list, I say we take no chances."

Mackenzie nodded. "I can't argue with that. Can you lose them?"

"Hold on."

I stomped the accelerator and the Mercedes surged into the intersection. I cranked the steering wheel, causing Mackenzie to yelp as we whipped onto a side street. I gave the car another burst of speed. Charging toward the center of the block, I cranked the steering wheel again. Tires screeching, the Mercedes fishtailed then rocketed into a narrow alleyway. After zipping past several dumpsters, I pulled tight to the alley wall, hit the brakes, and killed the engine. The line of dumpsters now hid my parked car from the main street.

"Are you crazy?" Mackenzie snapped. "You almost—"

"Wait."

I peered out at the side mirror, which gave me a perfect view of the alley's entrance. After a good minute and zero sign of the black SUV, I settled back in my seat. "Looks like we lost it."

"Great," Mackenzie said. "I mean, if that SUV really was following us."

"It was."

"If you say so."

I shot her a look. "Better safe than dead, right?"

"Not if you wrap us around a damn lamppost."

I laughed, restarted my car, and drove out of the alleyway.

Mackenzie couldn't help laughing with me.

Chapter 22

Just to play it safe, Jackson decided not to park his Mercedes in the underground garage. As we walked the short distance to Jackson's loft, we both remained vigilant, taking turns looking over our shoulders, scanning our surroundings. Whoever had been following us appeared to have vanished.

We rode an elevator to the top floor of a building that looked as if it had been recently renovated. The eight-unit complex had a modern angular look with lots of glass and chrome accents. Definitely way nicer than my town house.

"Wow," I said, when Jackson unlocked his front door and showed me inside. "This place is so Jackson Jones."

His face scrunched up. "I would ask you what you mean by that, but I don't think I want to know."

"It means this place is just like I thought it would be."

I surveyed the room and spotted a flat-screen TV even bigger than Prentice's. Jackson's leather sofa was almost as long and likely as expensive as the one in the office of the junior crime boss. The stark white walls were a perfect complement to the bamboo floors. There wasn't much furniture and only a couple of art pieces on the walls. The most impressive feature of Jackson's loft was its twenty-foot vaulted ceiling. The open space gave the room a majestic feeling.

"All you have to do is add a few touches of gold and Prentice won't have a thing on you."

"I'm going to ignore you and go grab a few things from the bedroom. Make yourself at home," Jackson said, heading toward a hallway.

Suddenly, he stopped mid-stride. "Strike that. Don't make yourself at home. Sit down and don't be nosing around in my stuff."

I laughed. "Sounds like you have something to hide."

Once Jackson left the room, I did exactly what he'd told me not to do. I nosed around. The kitchen, of course, had all the latest top-of-the-line appliances: an air fryer, a Ninja blender, a high-end latte machine that had to have cost more than a grand, as well as a couple of stainless-steel contraptions I couldn't identify.

I opened the refrigerator to find next to nothing. A pizza box, some dried-up fruit in the vegetable bin, a couple of beers, and several Styrofoam containers of half-eaten food. Typical bachelor fare.

A sliding glass door led out onto a small balcony. Jackson would've had a decent view if it hadn't been for the crappy motel standing between him and the Pacific Ocean. When I angled my head just right, I could see a sliver of the dark waters of Venice Beach. I walked back inside and zeroed in on the framed pictures sitting on his credenza. I picked up a photograph of Jackson and his daughter. She was adorable and had Jackson's broad smile and his nose. I chuckled when I saw that Jackson had cut someone out of the photo, most likely his ex-wife.

Pulling open one of the drawers, I was surprised to find a photo of Jackson from his LAPD days. He looked quite handsome in his uniform. I wondered if he missed being a cop. To be forced out of a job you loved for doing the right thing had to be hard. I'm glad Jackson turned in his dirty partner. Although I enjoyed teasing him about being a prima donna, what he did spoke volumes about the kind of man he was.

I heard Jackson rolling his luggage down the hallway, so I quickly shoved the photograph back into the drawer, stepped over to the balcony, and pretended to be taking in the nonexistent view.

When I turned back around and saw Jackson dragging two large suitcases behind him, I started cracking up.

"What's so funny?"

"Where do you think you're going with all that? Looks like you're planning on moving in. Permanently."

"You wish."

"I'm serious. You've packed enough clothes for a month. What all do you have in there?"

"Just a few necessities."

"Like what?"

"I hate washing clothes, so I had to bring multiple pairs of underwear, plus some jeans, three pairs of slacks, three shirts, and a couple of T-shirts. I brought one pair of dress shoes and two pairs of tennis shoes. And, of course, a nice suit and tie in the event the occasion calls for it. I also have my toiletries, two bottles of cologne, and my hair care products."

"Cologne? What kind of hair care products?"

"Mousse and coconut oil spray. Keeps my hair soft to the touch just the way the ladies like it."

I laughed. "You barely even have any hair."

Jackson slowly brushed his palm from his forehead to the nape of his neck. "Admit it. You love the way I take care of my crown. Wanna feel?"

I rolled my eyes.

"When I went to Paris for the summer, all I carried was one small suitcase and a backpack."

"Well, that's you and this is me."

"I don't have space for all that. Can't you get it down to one bag?"

"No, I can't. I don't like to scrunch up my clothes when I pack. That helps avoid wrinkles. But if you're volunteering to iron all my stuff . . ."

"You're definitely smoking something if you think I'm ironing your clothes. No, seriously."

"I need everything in here," Jackson protested.

"I doubt you can even get both of those bags in your car."

"You let me worry about that. You just—"

Jackson jerked his head toward the front door.

"Did you hear that?" he whispered.

"Nope," I said, still focused on his overpacked bags. "Didn't hear a thing."

"Be quiet," he said, his tone serious.

As Jackson started tiptoeing toward the door, I stiffened. This time I heard it. Someone was fiddling with the doorknob. It sounded as if they were trying to pick the lock.

Without a word between us, Jackson quickly moved away from the door as we both pulled out our guns and took cover. He ducked behind the couch, while I dashed into the hallway, keeping the front door in my line of vision. As we waited for the intruder to enter, my heart was beating double time. It had to be the masked man. If he was bold enough to break into Jackson's loft, that meant he was determined to kill us. We were not about to let that happen.

The instant the door swung open, Jackson and I simultaneously sprang from our hiding places, our guns aimed at the door and poised to fire.

"Don't move!" Jackson yelled.

For several seconds, time stopped, then morphed into a slow-motion haze of confusion. High-pitched screams reverberated throughout the room, piercing my ears, sending my already racing pulse even higher. Jackson and I quickly lowered our guns, shaken but immensely relieved. There was no intruder.

Robin and Nicole, Jackson's ex-wife and daughter, stood just inside the doorway, clutching each other, the fear etched in their faces amplified by the tremor in their bodies.

Chapter 23

JACKSON

The sight of my terrified baby girl staring down the barrel of my Glock stopped my heart.

I nearly dropped the weapon as I fumbled to get it back into my holster and rushed to Nicole. I pulled her trembling body into a tight hug. "I'm sorry, baby. I'm so sorry."

Mackenzie also repeatedly apologized as she put away her weapon.

Robin glared at me like she wanted to rip my head off, and she might be able to do it too. Her second home was the gym. "Seriously, Jackson?" she yelled.

I raised a hand, gesturing for Robin to postpone the fireworks while I focused on my daughter. Nicole was thirteen and blossoming into a beautiful young woman, but in my eyes she was still a little girl. "I know that must've been really scary," I said to Nicole. "But I would never hurt you. Are you okay?"

Before Nicole could respond, Robin unleashed another volley. "Don't be stupid. Of course she's not okay. You nearly killed us. You and that woman."

"That's Mackenzie. My partner."

"I'm so sorry," Mackenzie said to Robin. "We thought someone was trying to break in."

"Exactly," I said to Robin. "Why didn't you use the intercom like always?"

"Why wasn't your car in your parking space?" Robin shot back. "We weren't sure you were home."

"I parked on the street."

"And why the hell would you do that?"

"Watch your language," I said. "Nicky doesn't need to hear that."

"She doesn't need a gun pointed in her face either!"

"Okay, okay," I said, taking a de-escalating tone. "Mackenzie has already explained that. We both apologized. And nobody got hurt."

"Thank god," Robin said, rolling her eyes.

I went on, "Now can you please explain to me what you're doing here?"

Robin cocked her head in utter disbelief, catching me off guard. *Did I say something wrong?* Then the sight of Nicole's dejected expression, coupled with the overnight bag at her side, delivered a gut punch of realization.

Smelling blood, Robin's eyes narrowed. "You forgot, didn't you?"

I winced and nodded. "Yeah, I did. Sorry."

A week ago, Robin asked if Nicole could stay with me for a couple of nights while she and her friends went to a spa in Palm Springs. I agreed without hesitation. I'd never pass up an opportunity to spend time with Nicky. In fact, I was looking forward to it. I even made plans to surprise her with Universal Studios VIP Tour tickets. You'd think the small fortune I spent would make Nicky's visit impossible to forget, but then Big Ced happened. Parleying with gangsters, fighting fake ninjas, and escaping exploding houses have a way of pushing everything else out of your mind. And forgetting Nicky's sleepover wasn't the worst part. With killers coming at me from all sides, Nicole being anywhere near me was a very bad idea. So, besides greatly disappointing my daughter, I now had to tell my hotheaded ex-wife that her girls' trip to Palm Springs would have to be postponed. Unless I handled this correctly, World War III was about to break out in Venice Beach, California.

Robin slowly shook her head at me, savoring her contempt. "How could you forget? I even called this morning to remind you. Try checking your voicemail sometimes," she scolded.

"You're totally right," I said, essentially baring my neck in hopes she'd settle down a bit. "Listen, could we talk in the bedroom? Alone?"

"What? Why? I have to get back home to finish packing."

"Please. It'll only take a minute. I promise."

For an uncomfortably long moment, Robin just stared at me, perhaps trying to read my soul. Finally, with a dramatic sigh, she said, "fine."

I said to Nicole and Mackenzie, "You two get to know each other. We'll be right back."

Offering a small smile, Nicole nodded. "Okay, Dad."

The instant I shut the bedroom door, Robin pointed a stern finger at me. "This is going to cost you."

"Wait. What?"

"I might not be a private eye," she said, "but I did notice your suitcases. All packed and ready to go. Is that why you forgot all about your family? Because you and your girlfriend are about to go on some vacation?"

"First of all, Mackenzie is not my girlfriend, and we're not going on a trip. We're caught up in a very dangerous case and it wouldn't be safe to have Nicole around."

"Yeah, yeah, yeah," she said, wagging her head. "Whatever. Like I said, if you want me to rearrange my plans it's going to cost you."

"Meaning?"

"Meaning, I'll have to get my sister to watch Nicky, which I won't allow her to do for free. Let's say three hundred a day."

"That's a bit much to watch your own niece," I groaned, "but okay."

"Oh, we're not done," Robin said. "I now have to drive Nicky all the way out to Lancaster, so I'll arrive late in Palm Springs."

"Not that late."

"Point is," she continued, "I'll be late for dinner. We have reservations at Melvyn's. Do you know how difficult it is to get reservations at Melvyn's?"

"Okay, okay. You want me to pay for your dinner too. Got it."

"Not just the dinner," she said, "my entire trip."

"Oh, come on, Robin."

"No, you come on," she countered. "I do not appreciate you screwing up my plans. If you want me to be okay with this . . . you make it okay. And anyway, you can afford it."

As much as I resented Robin's shakedown, a part of me felt relieved that a full-on knock-down drag-out could be averted with just my signature on a check. Besides, she was right, the cost of her Palm Springs jaunt wouldn't put a dent in the money I'd score from the Keane case. "All right," I said with a defeated nod. "Just send me a bill or something, with receipts, of course."

She made a face. "What? Why can't you just Zelle me now? You don't trust your ex-wife?"

"Make it itemized receipts."

"Fine."

"Are we done?"

Robin frowned. "Not quite. You still have to tell Nicky. She's been looking forward to spending time with you for a week. It's all she talks about."

Those words stung far more than the money Robin had extorted from me.

"I'll make it up to her somehow," I said.

"You tell her that far too often," Robin said, "but you do always keep your word. I'll give you that."

"I'll take whatever I can get."

"Let me get her," Robin said, her voice softer now. She opened the bedroom door and called Nicole. When Nicole appeared in the doorway, she was still holding her overnight bag.

"Come in," Robin said to Nicole. "Your father has something to tell you."

Nicole approached me wearing a brave smile. She clearly knew what was coming. "Yeah, Dad?"

I swallowed hard and found the words. "Look, baby, something's come up with work. Something unexpected. So your mom's going to take you to your aunt's house instead. I'm really sorry and I promise that I will make this up to you. Okay?"

There were no tears, or glares, or huffing and puffing. Nicole just frowned and said, "It's okay, Dad. I understand."

Then she threw her arms around me and gave me a big, long hug. I'm not sure why. Perhaps because of the tears welling up in my eyes.

Chapter 24

MACKENZIE

As we drove up Lincoln Boulevard, toward my town house in Inglewood, Jackson was still seething from the dressing-down he'd received from Robin. For most of the drive, I left him alone to cool off. But in the end, I couldn't resist needling him.

"It was nice to finally meet Nicole," I said. "She is so sweet. She's basically your mini-me."

Jackson smiled. "That she is."

"And Robin's pretty, but she's definitely a piece of work. I couldn't believe she thought we were dating. Are you sure she's not still in love with you?"

Jackson stared straight ahead, refusing to respond. But I wasn't giving up.

"I could hear her yelling at you. You should ask her not to do that in front of your daughter. I could tell it upset her."

Jackson took his eyes off the road to glare at me for a few seconds. "You need to find something else to talk about." His tone was solemn.

"I've always wondered what kind of women you were into," I persisted. "I guess you like 'em feisty."

"You and my ex have a lot in common," Jackson shot back.

"That's not funny."

"I'm not trying to be funny."

Now it was my turn to go mute.

"Don't you want to know how?" Jackson prodded.

"No, because I'm nothing like her."

"Well, since you started down this road, I'm going to finish the trip. First, you're both headstrong."

I whipped my head in his direction. "What the hell does that mean?"

"It means you both spend too much time beating your chest and trying to act like you don't need anyone else. I just want to complement your life, not take it over. But you two make everything a competition."

"Excuse me for knowing how to take care of myself," I said, heat inching up my neck. "I'm not some damsel-in-distress type."

"That's exactly what I'm talking about. Take the chip off your shoulder."

"Screw you."

Jackson grinned excitedly. "Okay. When?"

I tried not to laugh, but I couldn't help it. "You're such a pig. I hate you."

Jackson chuckled. "No, you don't. You adore me. You wanna hear the other similarities between you and Robin?"

"Absolutely not."

"Okay, since you asked, I'll tell you. Both of you are smart as hell, which I really dig. You're also loyal and a lot of fun."

I was surprised by Jackson's compliments. "If Robin had those qualities, what went wrong?"

He shrugged. "I don't know. We just grew apart. I had a tough time when I was going through all that crap with the department. I should've opened up to her. Instead, I shut her out."

I let the silence linger for a while.

"You two certainly produced an amazing kid," I said.

"Robin has sole custody. Our divorce battle was getting pretty nasty, and I just got tired of fighting her on it. Besides, she knows that if she ever tried to keep my daughter from me, there'd be hell to pay. Bottom line, she's a great mother to Nicky and—"

Jackson's eyes darted to the rearview mirror. I instinctively turned around to see what had attracted his attention.

"We're being followed again," Jackson said, sitting more erect and gripping the steering wheel tighter.

"You're right." I spotted what appeared to be the same black SUV that followed us earlier. And this time it was practically tailgating us. "They're not even trying to be stealthy about it either."

After the attack on Vincent in the hospital and Yolonda's vicious murder, we were still on edge, knowing that we could very well be the next victims.

"Hold on," Jackson said. He cut a screeching hard U-turn in the middle of the street. The SUV immediately copied the maneuver and stayed on our tail. As we approached the intersection at Centinela and La Cienega, the light turned yellow. Jackson slowed inches from the intersection, quickly checked the cross traffic, then stomped the accelerator, speeding through the red light.

Suddenly, there were flashing lights from atop the SUV.

"They're cops," I said.

"Maybe," Jackson replied. "It could be a trick."

He hesitated, then pulled over to the curb in front of Phillips Barbecue. As two men in sports jackets exited the SUV, Jackson took out his gun and wedged it between his seat and the center console. Mine was already in my hand, which was resting in the side pocket of the passenger door.

Jackson rolled down the window a few inches.

"LAPD," said one of the men, flashing his badge. "Lieutenant Gooden wants to see you. Please follow us."

Relieved, I let go of my gun, leaving it in the side pocket.

"Are we under arrest?" Jackson asked.

The man grinned. "No, but you could be."

"For what?"

"Running that red light."

"That's not an arrestable offense."

"It is when I smell alcohol on your breath. Perhaps you're driving under the influence."

"And perhaps you're full of shit," Jackson fired back.

The other detective, who was much taller, stepped forward and peered down into the car. "Look, asshole, stop giving us a hard time. Just do as you're told."

"Excuse me, but I'm not five years old. Unless you're arresting me, I'm not following you anywhere."

This was about to get out of hand. I needed to do something to defuse the situation.

"Hey, guys," I said, leaning over to make eye contact. "Mark is a personal friend of mine."

Jackson loudly guffawed. "Give me a break."

"He won't like the way you're handling this," I continued, ignoring Jackson's reaction. "If we're not under arrest, we're not going with you. Please tell Mark I'll give him a call later."

The two men stepped away to speak to each other out of our earshot.

"*Mark is a personal friend of mine*," Jackson mimicked in a high, whiny voice. "*Tell Mark I'll give him a call later.*"

"Stop acting jealous," I said. "I needed to say whatever I had to say to make sure you didn't get us both shot."

"Those punks aren't going to shoot anybody. They're your new boyfriend's flunkies. That's why they're on babysitting duty. Look at 'em. Their feeble brains are incapable of figuring out what to do next."

The taller officer stepped back up to the window. "We're going to ask you one more time. Are you willing to follow us at the request of Lieutenant Gooden?"

"And I'm going to tell you one more time," Jackson said. "We're not following you anywhere."

The detective's jawline hardened. He was about to say something, but apparently thought better of it and simply trudged back to his car.

Chapter 25

JACKSON

Wow, this is nicer than I thought," I said as I wheeled my Mercedes into Mackenzie's carport. She lived in a complex of attached Mediterranean-style town houses. Earth-toned stucco, red roof tiles, arched windows and doorways, and loads of homey charm. The landscaping fronting Mackenzie's unit was noticeably tidier than her neighbors', although she never struck me as the green-thumb type.

Mackenzie cocked her head accusingly. "Why nicer than you thought? Because it's in Inglewood?"

This question blindsided me. Massive gentrification was changing Inglewood just like it was transforming other predominantly Black communities around the country.

"Are you kidding me?" I said. "You need at least a mil to buy a house in Inglewood these days. Your town house is tight. Hell, I could almost live here."

Mackenzie laughed.

"Of course, that just goes for the exterior," I went on. "We both know you're decorating disabled, so, to be honest, I'm kinda nervous about going inside."

"Fine," Mackenzie said with a shrug. "You can always sleep out here in the car." Then she climbed out and slammed the door behind her.

A moment later, Mackenzie stood by her front door, hands planted on her hips, staring as I parked my suitcases and wandered into her living room. Her hooded gaze practically dared me to make a wisecrack.

Her place was almost exactly as I imagined. Thoughtful and tasteful yet lacking in any real style. Functional and spare. Everything, including the open kitchen area, was insanely neat and clean, as if she employed a live-in maid.

"Well?" she said. "I gave you the business about your apartment. Your turn, I guess."

"I'll just say this place is very . . . you."

She frowned. "Okay. I'm not sure if that's good or a dig, but—okay."

"There is one thing that bugs me, though."

"What?"

"Where the hell is your TV?"

The wall opposite her uncomfortable-looking sofa had plenty of room for a good-sized flat screen; instead, three framed paintings occupied the space.

"Prepare yourself for a shock," she said. "I got rid of my TV."

I laughed. "Yeah, right. Seriously, where is it?"

"Jackson, I'm serious. If there's something I want to watch, I have my laptop or my phone."

I winced and said, "You don't like Chinese food and you don't own a TV. I'm sorry, but I don't think our partnership is going to work out."

"Stop it," she said, laughing. "I need wine. Want some scotch?"

"Wait, you actually have scotch?"

"You want some or not?"

"What kind? Never mind. Yeah. Sure."

While Mackenzie prepared our drinks in the kitchen, I plopped down on the sofa. The firm cushions were not butt-cheek friendly, and the throw pillows could double as weapons.

In no time, Mackenzie returned with our drinks and sat down next to me.

I patted the cushion between us. "You really expect me to sleep on this park bench?"

"Absolutely," she said. "A firm surface is great for your back." Then she raised her glass and said, "Here's to dodging explosions—"

"And ex-wives," I added.

We clinked glasses and sipped our drinks.

Mackenzie sighed and settled back on the sofa. "So, tomorrow. Bakersfield, right?"

She was right to get back to business. We were in a world of trouble and needed to remain focused. Vincent Keane's estranged daughter, Rebecca, was now our best lead. With any luck she'd hold the key to unraveling the mess we were in.

"Yup, Bakersfield," I replied with a nod. "And we should leave right after the morning rush hour to avoid turning a two-hour drive into five hours. Let's just hope no one gets there before we do."

"Considering the drive, should we call Rebecca first to arrange a meeting?"

"Not a good idea," I said. "We don't know how deep this beef with her dad goes. If she knows why we're coming she might—"

"Yeah," Mackenzie said. "Turn into a ghost."

"Exactly," I said, "but we should call using a cover. Just to make sure she'll be there."

"I have an idea," Mackenzie said, perking up. "Let's get Nadine to make the call. She'd love to be more involved and she'd be good at it."

Mackenzie knew I wasn't keen on dragging my cousin into the quicksand, but Nadine making a simple phone call should be harmless enough. And Mac was right, Nadine was mentally nimble and had a way with words. I had no doubt she'd do a great job. When I told Mackenzie I agreed with her idea she bounced in her seat a little.

"Nadine will be thrilled," she said.

Setting aside business until morning left room for a titillating idea to slink into my head. An idea that brought a mischievous smile to my face.

"What?" Mackenzie asked. "Why are you smiling like that?"

After a slow sip of my scotch I said, "I believe I owe you something."

"What?"

"The full treatment, remember?"

Mackenzie's eyes widened. "You mean a massage? Now?"

I shook my head. "The full treatment is much more than a mere massage."

"I'm still waiting to find out what it is exactly."

"Come on," I said. "Be adventurous. And if you say no, Roxy is not going to be happy."

"Hmmm." Mackenzie took a sip of wine, then scrunched up her face as she thought about it. Finally, she asked, "What would I have to do?"

"Nothing much. Just get naked and lie down on your bed. Oh yeah, and cover yourself with a towel, of course."

"Naked?" Mackenzie gave me a look. "I don't think so."

"What? You don't trust me? Or maybe you don't trust yourself."

"You wish. How about just a shoulder massage? Like you gave me when we were stuck at that cabin." She rubbed the back of her neck. "My neck is tighter than a rubber band."

She hopped up from the couch and moved to one of the kitchen chairs. "We can do it in here."

"Okay. But you're the one missing out."

I marched over to one of my suitcases and took out a bottle of massage oil. "Take off your top. Your bra too."

Mackenzie hesitated, then pointed a finger at me. "No funny stuff."

She removed her top, revealing a lacy beige bra. I was about to remark how sexy it was, but thought better of it. Instead of taking it off, too, she slid both straps down her arms.

I didn't sweat it. After this massage, she'd be begging me for the full-body treatment.

Pouring oil into my palms, I rubbed them together to warm up the oil, then gently gripped her shoulders. Mackenzie instantly tensed, then relaxed as my fingers delved into the pressure points along her neck and shoulders.

"That feels amazing," she moaned.

My fingers moved down her upper arms, then back up to her shoulders and long, sexy neck. Being a masseur is challenging work. But exploring Mac's body like this was just as pleasurable for me as it was for her.

My thumbs pressed the area behind her ears, then massaged her temples. "You really are good at this. Maybe I do want the full treatment."

Surprised that she'd relented so quickly, I hesitated. Once Mac was naked, I wasn't sure I'd be able to restrain myself. "Okay. Let's move this into the bedroom," I said.

Mackenzie rose from the chair just as the doorbell chimed.

"Are you expecting anyone?" I asked.

Mackenzie shook her head as she pulled her bra straps up and wiggled back into her top. "Absolutely not."

I reached for my gun. "I'll get it."

"Wait," Mackenzie said, reaching for her phone. "Let me check the Ring cam."

The instant she pulled up the app, surprise spread across her face.

"So who is it?" I asked.

"It's not good." She turned her phone to reveal video of Lieutenant Gooden standing at her doorstep, reaching for the bell again.

It chimed once more.

"Damn," I said, holstering my weapon. "Better go answer before your boyfriend shoots down the door."

"Don't start."

Moments later Lieutenant Good & Plenty, sporting another pricey suit, stood in Mackenzie's living room looking like a cover model for *Detective's Quarterly*. He griped a bit about the way we blew off his two cronies earlier, but that wasn't the real reason for his visit. He asked, "Were you two in the Monterey Park area today?"

The cologne-reeking snake already knew the answer to that question and was making a clumsy attempt to lay a trap. Thankfully, Mackenzie was on to him as well. We both nodded, then I said, "Yeah. Actually, we were. We went to talk to one of our clients. Why do you ask?"

"And what's this client's name?"

"You know we can't reveal that," Mackenzie said. "Privilege. What's this about?"

"This is about a house exploding . . . and a murder."

Mackenzie and I both feigned surprise.

"That's horrible," I said. "Sounds like you have a lot of work to do. So what are you doing here?"

"I'm here because the woman who perished in that explosion was connected to Vincent Keane. And you two are connected to

Keane. Also, your vehicle was identified in traffic cam videos near the explosion. That's quite a coincidence, don't you think?"

"Hold on," I said. "Are you saying we were on the same block as the explosion, because yeah, that would be one hell of a coincidence."

"Oddly enough," Lieutenant Gooden said, "all the footage from video cameras in the immediate area was scrubbed clean. So no, I can't place you two at the scene, but—"

"Come on," Mackenzie interrupted. "You really think Jackson and I did that? Really?"

The detective sighed and shook his head. "No, I don't. But I do think you know something about it. Also, I'm hoping that what happened today shows you two just how dangerous your new friends are."

"New friends?" Mackenzie said. "Our only new friend is you, Mark. And it's really nice how you're looking out for us."

Mackenzie's flirting made me want to hurl, but I could see her ploy was having the desired effect.

"I just don't want you to get hurt," Gooden said, his eyes fixed solely on Mackenzie.

"I appreciate you," Mackenzie said with a smile. Then, for a lingering moment, as they made eyes at each other, it was as if I wasn't even in the room.

Unable to stand it a second longer, I said to Lieutenant Gooden, "Hey, there's a mad bomber out there. Shouldn't you get back to your beat?"

He glanced at his watch. "Actually, I'm off duty." Then, to Mackenzie, "I do have to go wrap up something, but after that I'm totally free. If you're not busy I'd love to take you out for a drink."

If you're not busy? It took everything I had not to shout in Gooden's face. This joker's a detective so he definitely noticed the drinks on the table. What the hell did he think Mackenzie and I were doing, playing Monopoly?

Damn, I hated him, and now I couldn't wait to see the look on his stupid face when Mackenzie sent his ass to rejection city.

"You mean tonight?" Mackenzie asked.

"Yes, in about an hour. Is it a date?"

I resisted the urge to rub my palms together. This was going to be so good.

"Sure, Mark," Mackenzie said. "That sounds nice. I can't wait."

I nearly fell over.

Chapter 26

MACKENZIE

I got a real kick out of Jackson's reaction when I sauntered out of my bedroom wearing a slinky, low-cut red dress. He was sitting on my living room couch, his arms folded, sulking like a two-year-old.

Jackson's eyes traveled slowly up from my red stilettos.

"I don't think I've ever seen you in makeup before," he said, his voice flat. "Are you actually wearing false eyelashes?"

I made a show of batting my lashes at him. "I just felt like dressing up tonight."

Walking over to a mirror near the door, I touched up my lips with my candy-apple-red lip gloss.

"I can't believe you're actually going out with that dude."

"I am. So get over it."

"There's nothing for me to get over. I couldn't care less. Have a good time."

"I plan to." I gave him a sexy wink on my way out of the door. "Don't wait up."

I'd agreed to meet Lieutenant Gooden at Post & Beam in Baldwin Hills. When I stepped inside the restaurant—intentionally ten minutes late—he did a double take.

"Damn, you look amazing." He leaned in to give me a hug.

"Thanks, Lieutenant. You clean up pretty good yourself."

"Please call me Mark."

He was wearing dark gray slacks and a short-sleeved silk shirt with a geometric print. Tall and trim, his well-kept body was all muscle. I suspected the lieutenant was at least ten years my senior, but his smooth angular jawline, striking green eyes, and warm smile made him look years younger.

Once we were seated, his eyes kept dropping to my cleavage. Despite that annoyance, he was surprisingly charming and easy to talk to.

"So," he said, after we'd agreed on the catfish nuggets and warm homemade cornbread for appetizers, "how'd you end up doing PI work?"

Before I could answer, he cut me off. "Wait, let me guess. Your father was a cop and you somehow found yourself interested in criminal justice."

I laughed. "Not even close. Both of my parents are lawyers. I started out as an investigative journalist and that interest somehow morphed into PI work."

He nodded. "Well, I've certainly heard good things about your skills. You should consider law enforcement. There're some amazing opportunities for women these days. I could certainly see you quickly rising through the ranks. I know a couple of female police chiefs, if you'd ever like to chat with them."

I vigorously swung my head from side to side. "No, thanks. I'm a bit of a renegade. I love the freedom of working for myself."

"If that's the case, how'd you end up joining ranks with pretty boy?"

I ignored the *pretty boy* comment and chuckled to myself. If the lieutenant only knew the myriad of nicknames Jackson had for him.

"We were thrown together on a missing-persons case that turned out to be pretty harrowing. And after surviving that ordeal, it just made sense to join forces."

He grimaced. "Is he the one who got you mixed up with Vincent Keane?"

"Who said I was mixed up with Keane?"

"C'mon. You didn't show up at Keane's hospital room just as he was being attacked by happenstance. You be real with me and I'll be real with you."

I smiled, propped my elbow on the table, and daintily rested my chin in my hand. "I'm always real."

"Tell me how you're involved with Vincent Keane? Who're you working for?"

"C'mon, Lieutenant, you know I can't share confidential client information with you."

"Okay, then," he said, continuing to press me. "I don't need to know who your client is. Tell me why were you at Big Ced's office the same time Bioff and Meza happened to be there. Did you meet with those guys too?"

"Nope," I lied.

"Look, I didn't just invite you to dinner because I think you're beautiful. We're here because I'm concerned about you. Those are some very dangerous people you're fooling with."

"I'm a big girl. I know how to take care of myself."

"I know how to take care of myself, too, but even I'd be leery about getting tangled up with those dudes. If you can't tell me who you're working for, at least tell me why you're interested in Keane."

"I can't do that."

He pursed his lips and his eyes hardened. "These guys are killers. You and your partner need to be very careful."

"I really appreciate your concern, Mark. Exactly what's so dangerous about Keane?"

"As I'm sure you know, he's a big-time con man with a criminal record longer than my arm. He should've been locked up years ago, but every time we were close to nailing him, he hired expensive attorneys and beat the system. But now, somebody wants him dead and I suspect you know why."

"Is Keane even still alive?" I said, ignoring his last statement.

"He's in a coma, but his doctors expect him to wake up any day now. We're eager to find out if that traffic accident was really an accident."

"You don't think it was?"

"Nope."

"You think it was a failed hit?" I asked.

"Probably."

Lieutenant Gooden smiled. "You do realize that I realize you're pumping me for information, right?"

I smiled and angled my head. "Am I?"

"I'm going to have to be very careful with you."

"So help a sister out," I said. "What can you tell me about why someone wants to kill Keane?"

He waggled a finger at me. "It doesn't work that way. If you wanna know what I know, I need to know what you know. Any exchange of information has to be a two-way street."

"It can be," I lied for the second time. "Has Keane had any visitors at the hospital?"

"Just one. A longtime friend, a guy named Tony. They played chess at Santa Monica's Chess Park for decades. He tried to visit Keane, but the uniform on duty turned him away since he wasn't family. But we checked him out."

"Does Tony have a last name?"

"Yep." The lieutenant grinned and tossed a catfish nugget into his mouth.

I waited, but he just kept chewing.

"So you're not going to share his last name?"

"Maybe. It depends on what you've got for me. What's your connection to Keane? Is he your client?"

"No," I said. "Keane definitely isn't my client."

"Then who is?"

"I wish I could tell you, but I can't."

"Okay then, why were you at Big Ced's office?"

I pursed my lips. "Sorry, that's confidential information too."

The lieutenant sighed and massaged the back of his neck. I could tell he was growing frustrated with me, which I didn't want to happen. He was right about this being a dangerous case we were working. After the threat from Prentice, it would be good for Jackson and me to have a direct line of communication with him.

"Look, Mark, at the moment I don't have *any* information I can share with you. But when I do, I will." I reached across the table and squeezed his forearm, giving him a closer view of my cleavage in the process. "I promise."

He ignored me, leaned back in his seat, and smiled. "You're really something else, young lady."

I winked. "I try to be."

Just then, the waitress interrupted to take our dinner orders. I chose the shrimp and grits, the lieutenant opted for the beef short ribs.

"Enough about Keane," I said, once the waitress had disappeared. "Let's talk about something else."

"Good idea. But first, I need a commitment from you."

I quietly sighed, expecting him to lecture me about being careful on the case.

"I wanna see you again," he said, taking me by surprise. "So how about it?"

My thoughts went straight to Jackson. He'd die if Lieutenant Gooden and I became an item. I had to stifle a laugh as I imagined the look on his face.

"I like that smile on your face," he said. "Does that mean the answer is yes?"

"Absolutely," I said. "I'd love to see you again."

Chapter 27

I resisted the urge to do some serious snooping around Mackenzie's town house while I waited for her to return from her date with Lieutenant Good-time. Instead, I just sat there in her living room watching YouTube and TikTok videos on my phone while sipping scotch.

I would've preferred to watch some TV, but along with being a neat freak it appeared that my new partner was a closet Luddite. One thing for certain, although Mackenzie had left me a blanket and pillow, there was no way I'd get a wink of sleep. Not just because of the rock-hard sofa. Just the thought of that playboy detective getting frisky with Mackenzie, especially while she wore that sexy red dress, jangled my nerves like a double shot of caffeine. Nope, scotch and crazy Karen videos would have to do until Mackenzie walked back through that front door.

Around nine, with still no sign of Mackenzie, a disturbing thought prompted me to set down my phone. She'd been gone for damn near three hours, more than enough time for a few drinks and to endure Gooden's boring stories. What the hell was taking so damn long? The way I figured it there were two possibilities. One,

Mackenzie was actually having a good time. Or two, she was having an incredibly good time. Was that possible? Would she really go back to his place?

I shook my head and laughed, then downed another gulp of scotch. Nope. No way. Mackenzie could never fall for a guy like that. But then again, why not? Gooden's handsome and fit and always smells good, kind of like—me. The only thing keeping Mackenzie and me from being together was the stupid hands-off pact we made before going into business together. Gooden, on the other hand, was fair game. Sure, Lieutenant Good-enough was a piss-poor substitute for Jackson Jones, but—maybe good enough was all Mackenzie needed right now.

For the last hour or so, trying to play it cool, I had restrained myself from texting Mackenzie for an update, but now—screw that.

I snatched up my phone and began typing, but stopped when I heard Mackenzie at the door.

When she entered and tossed her keys on a side table, I couldn't stop myself from crossing my arms and addressing her like a perturbed dad. "Well, it's about time, young lady. You've been gone for almost three hours."

"I know you're joking," Mackenzie said, as she began to remove her high heels, "but I am so tired. Sweet of you to wait up for me, though. What'd you do all night, watch TikTok?"

"No," I lied. "I watched a documentary about police corruption."

"Really? Was it any good?"

Mackenzie's hair and makeup were pretty much undisturbed, that was a good sign, but I couldn't help noticing that she seemed to be steering our conversation away from the elephant in the room.

"The documentary was fantastic," I said. "How was Lieutenant Good-stuff?"

"Don't start," she said with a chuckle, then she joined me on the sofa. She sighed and reclined. "It's so nice to be home."

That's when I knew she was messing with me. "Come on," I said. "Are you going to tell me what happened on the date or not?"

She smirked at me. "You really are jealous. Is that the real reason you couldn't sleep?"

"Are you having fun?"

"I am having fun. Seeing you all huffy over me."

"How much did you have to drink, exactly?"

"Don't change the subject, jealous boy. I didn't hear a denial."

I shrugged and lied again. "I might be a little jealous."

"Just a little?"

"A teeny tiny little bit."

Mackenzie leaned in closer and whispered, "You're not fooling anyone."

"Are you done having your fun?" I said. "Can you tell me about the date now?"

Mackenzie sighed. "It wasn't a date, silly. It was reconnaissance. And that's all it was."

"You mean between you two playing footsie beneath the table and whispering sweet nothings you actually learned something?"

"That's exactly what I mean," Mackenzie said. "Turns out Mr. Keane has a BFF that he's been playing chess with every day for decades. Sounds to me like a more promising lead than that angry daughter all the way out in Bakersfield."

"I agree. Does this chess player have a name?"

"Tony something. But he shouldn't be hard to track down. Gooden wouldn't tell me his last name."

This tidbit brought a smile to my face. "I guess you really didn't sleep with Gooden."

She shook her head. "Definitely not . . . but, wow, he's a fantastic kisser."

I shrugged. "Hey, if that's what floats your boat, go for it. The more I think about it, the guy does seem like your type."

"I don't have a type," Mackenzie shot back. "And I don't like mixing business with pleasure."

I smiled. "Only time will tell."

Chapter 28

MACKENZIE

I didn't realize how exhausted I was until I collapsed onto my bed, still fully dressed.

Jackson was nestled underneath a blanket on my living room couch. I could hear D'Angelo's melodic voice drifting through my closed bedroom door. I had a sneaking suspicion that Jackson had intentionally cranked up the volume, expecting me to storm into the room demanding that he turn the music down. But I was too bushed to even plant my feet on the floor.

Dinner with Lieutenant Gooden turned out to be a soothing end to a nerve-racking day. Our time together was a much-needed reprieve, almost making me forget that deadly explosion, the looming threat from Prentice, and being summoned to the police station by two inept detectives.

I found myself pleasantly surprised by how much I enjoyed the lieutenant's company. He was not only attractive, but very warm and easy to talk to. I usually shied away from guys in law enforcement. They tended to be a bit too macho for my taste. But Mark, like Jackson, had a soft side behind the manly veil he donned every day.

Maybe it was time to reconsider my moratorium on men. But

then again, the lieutenant was a great contact for a PI to have. If we got involved and it didn't work out, I'd lose that connection. And to be honest, it probably wouldn't work out.

In the early days of a relationship, men were always amazing. However, over time, their quirks would inevitably surface. Guys who had a controlling nature bugged me the most. Admittedly, I wasn't always the easiest person to get along with. I was too much of a loner to fully allow someone into my world. Men always seemed to want more from me than I was prepared to give. What I needed was a man who would allow me to be myself. Someone who truly understood me.

Like Jackson.

I'd never admit that to him, but it was true. I was still reeling from that compliment he gave me in the car. *Smart. Loyal. A lot of fun.*

Jackson was precisely the kind of guy I could vibe with. He was intelligent, caring, funny, and sexy as hell. His only drawback was being quite the prima donna.

It didn't matter. We were business partners now. Taking things further would be a colossal mistake, perhaps an even bigger mistake than getting involved with Lieutenant Gooden.

I forced myself into a sitting position. My life was such a train wreck. I had no idea what I really wanted, and even if I did, I'd probably be too afraid to go after it.

Climbing out of bed, I slipped off my dress and slipped into a long T-shirt. I turned off the lamp on the nightstand and buried myself underneath my thick comforter.

Too bad Lieutenant Gooden had dropped by when he did. Who knows what would've happened. I closed my eyes, savoring the thought of Jackson's firm hands rubbing my shoulders, then slowly caressing their way down my back in long, gentle strokes.

I stared up into the darkness, frustrated with myself for always being so cautious. We were adults. What if we got together and really connected? But then again, what if we didn't?

My brother was right, I was way too uptight. I deserved a night of pleasure. A fine-ass man I was undeniably attracted to was just a few feet away on the other side of that door. And there was no question that Jackson's desire for me was just as strong as mine was for him. So why were we sleeping in separate rooms?

I should rip off this T-shirt and stalk naked into the living room. There would be no need for words. Jackson would look up at me, his smile widening as we melted into each other's arms. When our lips touched, it would ignite a passion so profound, we'd ravish each other like two starving animals. We'd fall to the couch and Jackson would kiss his way down my body.

I took a long, deep breath, hoping to quell the intense surge of desire coursing through my body. Jackson and I were in the middle of a dangerous case that could cost us our lives. The masked man was probably someplace plotting his next attack on us right now. This was not the time to be thinking about getting busy with my new partner. Our priority had to be staying alive. The best way to do that was to remain focused and vigilant.

We needed to find this Tony guy and pray he could lead us to Keane's evidence so we could swiftly wrap up this case. Only then could I entertain thoughts of Jackson or Lieutenant Gooden or whoever.

Despite the exhaustion that consumed my body, my mind would not stop spinning with thoughts of Jackson. I sat up in bed, flicked the lamp back on, and grabbed a novel from the nightstand. A good mystery usually did the trick, lulling me to sleep after just a few pages. Opening the book, I removed the bookmark and attempted to immerse myself in the story.

A soft knock on the door made me flinch.

"Jackson, is that you?" I asked, tensing as I placed the book on the bed beside me.

"Of course it is." The door eased open and Jackson stuck his head inside. "Who else would it be?"

"It's late. What do you want?"

I could barely make out his face in the dimly lit room. "Um . . . I was just . . ."

"It's late," I said again, fearing that if he didn't leave soon, I might lose control and throw myself at him. "Spit it out. What do you want?"

Jackson hesitated, then continued. "I was just wondering if it'd be okay if I slept with you tonight?"

Chapter 29

JACKSON

Mackenzie's reaction was not at all what I expected. Her bedroom was dimly lit, so maybe it was the shadows playing tricks. Her eyes were heavy-lidded, her head tilted invitingly, her hands clawed the bedsheets. She looked ready to jump my bones. Then, in the wink of an eye Mackenzie was back to her old aloof self.

She crossed her arms. "Excuse me?"

"Relax," I said. "I'm talking actual sleep. Nothing else. That IKEA torture device you call a sofa is killing me. Did I ever tell you I have back problems?"

"No. Never."

"I have back problems."

She drew her crossed arms in tighter. "That's pretty vague . . . and convenient."

"This isn't a move," I said, "if that's what you're implying. I really can't sleep on that thing."

"Fine," she said, moving to get up. "*I'll* take the sofa."

"Why?" I said. "Your bed's big enough for both of us. I'll sleep on one side, you on the other. We'll never even rub elbows."

"Or anything else," she said sharply.

"Exactly. So, what do you say? Please."

She pinned me with earnest eyes. "Jackson, considering our past—and you know what I mean—don't you think us sleeping in the same bed is a bit too tempting?"

I knew exactly what she meant, and she had a fair point, but for some reason I was now determined to share a bed with Mackenzie Cunningham. Maybe simply to prove to her that we could resist temptation. Or maybe I secretly hoped that something actually would spark once we were beneath those covers. In other words, at that moment I wasn't quite sure which brain I was working with.

"Here's the thing," I said to Mackenzie. "A little while ago you were going to let me give you the special treatment. That would've been way more tempting. Believe me."

"Oh really?"

"Point is . . . this will be just two mature adults sleeping side by side."

Mackenzie pursed her lips, pondering the question. Finally, she sighed and said, "Fine, but no—"

"I know," I said. "No funny business."

"That, too, but I was going to say no spooning."

"How about some good forking?"

"You know what—"

"Sorry, I couldn't resist."

Mackenzie moved to the right side of her bed, making room for me. "Come on before I change my mind."

"Actually, do you mind if I sleep on the right side? That's kinda my side."

"Not in my bedroom it isn't."

"Fair enough." I rounded to the left side of the bed and slipped beneath the blankets beside her. The mattress was firm, of course, but nothing close to that dreaded sofa. Her high-thread-count bed-ding was soft and infused with a soothing vanilla aroma that had an immediate settling effect on my entire body.

"Um, you okay over there?" Mackenzie asked.

"Yup."

She killed the lamp on her bedside table.

We lay there, side by side, on our backs, in silence, staring up at the ceiling. Finally, I whispered, "A bitcoin for your thoughts."

"I'm trying to decide if I should lay some pillows in between us."

I chuckled, then said, "Like that would stop me."

"FYI, I keep a gun in my nightstand."

"Noted. Hey, can I ask you a question?"

"Ask me tomorrow," she said rolling onto her side to face away from me. "Go to sleep."

"Real quick. When I asked if I can sleep with you, did you think I was serious, because for a second there—"

"Finish that sentence," she said, "and you'll be sleeping in a motel."

"Got it. Just one more little thing."

"No more things," she groaned. "Go to sleep. Please."

"I can't sleep without it."

"What is it? What?"

"Can you sing me a sweet lullaby?"

"Good night, jerk."

"Nighty night."

Chapter 30

The Santa Monica Chess Park was a modest collection of rickety picnic benches, weathered chessboards, and a mismatch of chess players who looked as worn as their equipment. We arrived at the park, which was a stone's throw from the Santa Monica Pier, around ten. As we approached the tables, we still had no clear strategy for how we would identify Vincent Keane's friend Tony.

We stood off to the side, amazed by the intensity of the games and the way the players were laser focused on their chessboards. Most of them appeared to be in their forties and fifties, but a couple could've passed for middle schoolers. Each table was equipped with a timer. After making a move, a player would slam the timer, which emitted a low ding. Consequently, a rhythmic pattern of dings filled the air every few seconds.

Jackson and I were the sole spectators at the moment. All around us, everyone else was totally engrossed in their game.

"Let's just call out his name and see who looks up," Jackson whispered to me.

"Sometimes, it's hard to believe you're actually a private investigator," I said.

"What's that supposed to mean? You have an easier way to identify him?"

"Of course I do." I pointed at a table a few yards away. "Tony's the guy over there with the scraggly gray beard and pot belly."

"And how do you know that?"

I tapped my index finger against my temple. "Because I'm brilliant."

Jackson twisted his lips. "Yeah, right."

"I'm serious. It's just deductive reasoning. Mark told me Keane and Tony have been playing chess here for decades. That guy's the only one old enough to fit the bill."

"You know it irks me when you call him Mark, right?"

"Really." I grinned and decided to do it again. "Well, that's what Mark told me."

Jackson folded his arms. "You're just guessing. It could also be that guy over there in the black T-shirt. He's certainly been around a few decades. And for all we know, Tony could be sitting at home watching the History Channel."

I shook my head as I started moving toward the bearded man's table. "I just have a feeling that he's our guy. But let's not interrupt him until the game is over."

"That could be a while."

I glanced over my shoulder at Jackson.

"Like I said, sometimes I'm stunned at what you do for a living." I tapped my temple again. "There are only four pieces left on their board. It won't be long at all."

I positioned myself to the left of the bearded player, and in a few swift moves, he hit the timer and called out, "Checkmate."

I immediately gave Jackson a satisfied smile.

"Whatever," he mumbled. "He still may not be our guy."

The bearded man stood up and stretched. He had to be pushing seventy, but moved like he was at least ninety. He had the look of a nutty professor. The hair on his head was as white and wiry as his ungroomed beard. His clothes could've used a good pressing. For a man who spent a lot of time playing chess under the bright sun, his skin was as pale as porcelain.

"Tony," I said, taking a step toward him, "do you have a second?"

The man peered at me over the rim of his reading glasses. "Maybe," he said in a gruff voice. "Depends on who's asking."

I smiled knowingly at Jackson.

"My name is Mackenzie and this is my partner, Jackson."

I extended my hand and Tony shook it. His frail-looking fingers delivered a surprisingly strong grip.

"We're here about your friend Vincent Keane."

"What about him?"

"Were you aware that he was in a really bad car accident?"

"Yep, found out a few days ago. When he didn't show up for our regular game, I tried to contact him, but he didn't pick up or call me back, which was unusual. Then I saw that news story about him being attacked in the hospital. Can you believe that shit? What is the world coming to?"

Tony's expression suddenly darkened. "Is Vincent okay? I tried to visit him, but they said I couldn't because I wasn't family. After that, I called the hospital to check on him every few days. Told them I was his brother."

"He's fine," Jackson said. "For now."

"Glad to hear that. He was one of my best law students and remains one of my best clients to this day."

"He's your client?" I asked.

Tony nodded. "I've handled his legal affairs for decades."

Jackson and I traded excited glances.

"So you were one of his professors at Southwestern Law School?" I asked.

"Sure was. Vincent was one of the brightest young legal minds I ever encountered. It's a shame he chose a different path."

"And what path was that?" Jackson said.

Tony laughed. "Perhaps you should tell me why you have me on the witness stand, young man."

"We're private investigators," Jackson said. "And we're hoping you might be able to help us find some information."

"What kind of information? And for whom?"

"For a client whose identity we can't disclose," Jackson said.

Tony's bushy eyebrows arched with skepticism. "Go on. I'm listening."

"Since you're Vincent's lawyer, would you happen to have a copy of his will?" I asked.

"Sure do," Tony said, picking his tooth with the long nail of his baby finger.

I struggled to tamp down my excitement. We were going to make it out of this case alive after all.

"We'd like to see it," Jackson said. "We think it might contain some information that's very important to our client."

Tony chuckled. "No can do. Vincent gave me very specific instructions. Nobody sees that will until he's dead. And as you just told me, he ain't dead yet."

"This could be a life-and-death matter," I said.

"The only life and death I care about," Tony said, "is Vincent's."

"Do you happen to know what's in his will?" Jackson asked.

"Nope. I didn't draft it. Vincent did it himself. Gave it to me in a sealed envelope. He even bought me one of those high-tech digital safes to keep it in. It's been locked away in my office ever since and that's exactly where it's staying."

"So you still practice law?" I asked.

"Not much. Just minor stuff for family and friends. But I still have a small office in Glendale."

"You're a solo practitioner?"

"Sure am. Tony Bonaducchi and Associates, LLP," he said proudly, then winked. "Never had any associates, though."

"There're some very dangerous people who want to get their hands on Vincent's will," Jackson said. "You could use a couple of friends like us. We can protect you. It's harmful to your health to have that will in your possession."

Tony spread his arms and chuckled again. "Look at me. You think I care about my health? Nobody's seeing that will until Vincent is dead. So tell your client no go."

It was clear that we'd run into a brick wall that could not be penetrated. Still, I continued to push.

"This is very serious. Vincent had dealings with some very shady people. The folks who want to see his will are ruthless. They'll stop at nothing to get it."

"Does that include your client?"

I decided to ignore his question. "You just need to be very careful."

"Understood," Tony said, though he appeared unfazed. "I'm well aware of the kind of hoodlums Vincent was mixed up with."

"It might be a good idea for you to get out of town," Jackson urged him.

"I'll give that some thought." Tony glanced at his watch. "My next game starts in twenty minutes. I need to take a leak. Anything else?"

Chapter 31

JACKSON

Leaving Chess Park and the Pacific Ocean behind, I drove my Mercedes east along Santa Monica Boulevard, headed to Roxanna's new place in Hancock Park.

About six months ago, courtesy of a well-armed hit squad gunning for Mackenzie and me, Roxy's gorgeous Beverly Hills mansion was shot to hell. Far too busy with day-to-day hacking hijinks to trifle with home repairs, Roxy simply dumped the place and snapped up a new one.

Following our meeting with Keane's pal Tony Bonaducchi, calculating our next move did not require the strategic prowess of a chess grandmaster. In fact, although extremely risky, what needed to be done was our only real option. We had to locate Tony's office, break in, crack his safe, and get our hands on Vincent Keane's will. Difficult? Absolutely. But not impossible. Especially when you have the right connections. A quick call to Roxanna, before we left Chess Park, confirmed that she could help engineer this mini-heist, and she urged us to come see her right away.

Mackenzie and I also decided to no longer share our to-do list with Prentice. There was clearly a leak in the underworld that led right to our cold-blooded masked competitor. If we were going to find Keane's stash first, not to mention keep breathing, we had to take every precaution to remain at least one step ahead of the game.

As we slid by the high-end boutiques and vintage shops of West Hollywood, stomach pangs reminded me that one of my favorite fast-food joints was just a few blocks away. Neither of us had eaten since morning.

"Let's grab some quick lunch," I said to Mackenzie. "Pink's is crazy close."

The expression that leaped onto her face suggested the unthinkable. Was it possible that Mackenzie Cunningham was a Pink's virgin?

"Hold up," I said. "You've never eaten at Pink's before?"

"Actually," she said, "I've been trying to avoid that place ever since I moved back home. I don't get it. People lining up for overhyped and overpriced meat tubes. Seems dumb to me."

Instead of kicking her out of my car, I squeezed the steering wheel and took a calming breath.

Pink's Hot Dogs was iconic. That beloved eighty-year-old shack near the corner of La Brea and Melrose was as much a Los Angeles landmark as the Griffith Observatory or the Venice Boardwalk. Locals and tourists alike lined up night and day eager to indulge in one of Pink's creatively themed nine-inch-long gourmet creations. Even an occasional Oscar winner has been spotted in the queue. The classic chili dog was the most popular offering, my personal favorite, but the menu also boasts specialties like curry dogs, pastrami dogs, and even an onion-ring-wrapped wonder called the Lord of the Rings. Not everyone likes hot dogs, I can force myself to accept that, but for Mackenzie to turn up her nose at the place without even giving it a chance was beyond irritating. She hates Chinese food, doesn't watch TV, and thinks hot dogs are beneath her. At this point I wouldn't be surprised if Mackenzie told me she hated *Star Wars*.

Making a mental note to bring up George Lucas's masterpiece later, I said to Mackenzie, "Listen, you maniac. Pink's are not just hot dogs. They're the best hot dogs in the entire world."

Mackenzie laughed. "Do you even hear yourself? You sound like a five-year-old."

"Come on," I said, "just give it a try. It's on me. And if you don't like it, I'll grill you a steak tonight. You do like steak, right?"

"Actually, I prefer salmon."

"Whatever. Is it a deal?"

Mackenzie sighed. "Fine. Let's go get us some meat tubes."

The roped-in line of customers outside Pink's was just right. Short enough to keep Mackenzie from whining, yet long enough for us to savor the aroma of sizzling hot dogs and grilling onions wafting from within.

Before long we had a tray of food and found seating at a small wobbly table on the back patio. We both ordered Diet Cokes and a side of fries. I went for the chili dog, of course, and encouraged Mackenzie to do the same, but she surprised me and ordered the LA Street Dog. Piled high with bacon strips, grilled peppers and onions, mushrooms, and jalapeños, this choice seemed a bit optimistic for a skeptical newbie, but when I questioned her choice she shrugged and said, "Hey, if I'm going to do this, I'm going to do it all the way."

Momentarily forgetting my chili dog, I stared as Mackenzie hoisted the heaping hot dog with both hands and took a huge bite. Fixings dripping down her fingers, cheeks still fat with food, Mackenzie mumbled, "Wow, this isn't bad."

"Does that mean you like it?"

She waved me off and took another huge bite. That was all the confirmation I needed. Perhaps there was hope for this crazy lady after all.

We didn't do much talking until our hot dogs and fries were gone and all that remained was to drain our drinks.

"It doesn't seem real, does it?" Mackenzie muttered between sips.

"What doesn't seem real?"

"Look at us, eating hot dogs and fries, chatting." Then she leaned forward and whispered, "In a few days we could be dead. I mean, really, what are we doing?"

I felt it, too, the threat of death looming in the back of my mind. "We're keeping ourselves sane," I told her. "Worrying night and day sure won't help."

"Are we really sane?" Mackenzie asked. "Is it sane to wait around to be killed?"

I put down my cup and leveled a stare at Mackenzie. "What are you saying?"

"Maybe we should run. I know, I know—but we're smart. If we put our minds to it, I know we can disappear. Start a new life."

I shook my head. "You don't really want to do that."

Mackenzie slumped back in her chair and sighed. "You're right. I'm sorry. I just—"

I placed my hand over hers and gave it a gentle squeeze. "Stop. Believe me, I thought about running as well. In fact, this conversation is way overdue. But here's the thing, you and I are going to get this done and get our lives back. Know why?"

"Why?"

"Because now that you're a Pink's fan, and we can chow down here every week, there's no way in hell we're leaving LA."

Mackenzie chuckled.

Hancock Park was just a quick five-minute drive from Pink's. The houses in the affluent and historic neighborhood were sprawling and expensive, damn near rivaling anything in Beverly Hills. Whenever I found myself navigating Hancock Park's wide, tree-lined streets, I'd often slow down to admire the grand Prohibition-era homes that give the area its unique charm.

It always felt as if I had traveled back in time, motoring through old LA during a period when men that looked like me, exploring an area like this, would be viewed with suspicion.

When you think about it, things hadn't really changed much.

Roxanna's address brought us to a striking Tudor-style mansion fronted by a perfect lawn. A redbrick walkway, flanked by trimmed hedges, stretched to an ornate front door.

As we made our way up the walk, Mackenzie said, "She sure loves big houses, huh?"

"Yes, she does. Roxanna came from nothing. Maybe this is how she compensates. I tell you one thing, that woman loves to indulge herself."

Right on cue, the front door flew open, and Roxanna emerged wearing pink Louis Vuitton silk pajamas, fuzzy pink Gucci slippers, and Bulgari cat eye glasses, also pink. I was unclear on the rules regarding mixing designers, but, as always, Roxy looked sexy as hell.

"*Moji miláčci*," she squealed, greeting Mackenzie and me with big hugs and kisses on both cheeks. "It is so wonderful to see you two." Then to Mackenzie, "Tell me. How was the special treatment? Wonderful, yes?"

"Um, we haven't done it yet?" Mackenzie said.

Roxanna wheeled on me and said sternly, "Jackson Jones, you must keep this promise." Somehow her thick Czech accent made her demand sound like a matter of life or death.

"I will, I will," I said. "We've just been kind of busy running for our lives."

Roxanna nodded. "Okay. Not a bad excuse."

I gestured to the house behind her. "I love your new place."

"Yeah," Mackenzie said. "It's . . . pretty impressive. I mean, wow."

"This is nothing," Roxanna said, grabbing Mackenzie's hand and tugging her toward the door. "Wait until you see inside."

Roxanna wasn't kidding—the interior was ridiculous. Vaulted ceilings, exposed beams, an elegant spiral staircase, and herringbone-patterned hardwood floors. What surprised me most was the period furniture: each piece looked like it belonged in a friggin' museum. Roxanna usually went for sleek and modern, bordering on garish, but this time capsule of a house was the complete opposite.

The way Mackenzie's head swiveled as she took in the place told me she was equally impressed.

"Roxy, this is amazing," I said. "I mean, really."

"Honestly," Mackenzie said, "I don't think I've ever been in a more beautiful home."

"Thank you so much," Roxy said, beaming. "And the best part— this is a Paul Williams house. The great Black architect, yes?"

Mackenzie gasped. "Oh my god. I've always wanted to experience a Williams house in person."

I'd never heard of this Paul Williams but judging by Roxy's evident pride and Mackenzie's awed reaction, he was clearly a big deal. The embarrassment of me knowing more about a hot dog stand than about a significant figure in Black history was too much "rag Jackson fuel" to give Mackenzie. For that reason, I decided to keep my ignorance to myself until I could google the brother and, to be safe, quickly change the subject.

"That's great, Roxanna," I said. "You can give us a full tour another time, but we should really get to work." I glanced around. "Where's your new command center?"

"No need for us to go in there," she said. Then she picked up a thick manila envelope from the coffee table and handed it to me.

"What's this?"

"Everything you need," she said. "Floor plans for Bonaducchi's office, alarm system schematics, passcodes, and detailed instructions on how to open his safe. Just study carefully and you're good to go. If something goes wrong, call me. But it won't. Easy as cake."

Mackenzie and I traded puzzled looks.

I held up the manila envelope. "All of that is in here?"

"Correct," Roxanna said. "I even put the patrol schedule for the local police. You are welcome."

"But how?" Mackenzie said to Roxanna. "We called you a little over an hour ago. How could you have compiled all this so fast?"

Roxanna laughed. "Mackenzie, *má milá*, in one hour I can collapse the power grid of an entire nation. I can siphon billions from a financial institution that believes it's invulnerable. I can pay thousands of hospital bills of people who have nothing. I can probably do all three with time to spare. In my business . . . an hour is an eternity. This safecracking mumbo jumbo stuff is nothing for me. Do you see now?"

A bit dazed, Mackenzie nodded and said, "Yeah—you are one very dangerous lady."

Chapter 32

MACKENZIE

We waited until nightfall before heading to the offices of Tony Bonaducchi and Associates, LLP. For most of the drive, my head was on a constant swivel, like a broken bobblehead doll, checking our surroundings. If the masked mystery man was on our tail tonight, I saw no sign of him. I even encouraged Jackson to make a few random turns just to ensure no one was following us.

For the record, Jackson and I weren't in the habit of breaking the law. But with our lives at stake, we had no choice. We needed to get a look at Vincent Keane's will, and breaking into Tony's safe was the only way to do that.

Roxanna's information about Tony's office proved to be remarkably accurate, so we didn't expect that breaking into the office would be much of a problem. Tony's storefront office along Glendale Boulevard, much like the man himself, was a bit of a relic. The one-story building even had a back entrance that bordered a wide, messy alley.

We parked a block away and I got out of the car first, pretending to be taking a leisurely late-night stroll. The back parking lot was empty, which was a relief. We knew little about Tony's office mates or their working hours. Roxanna had found no cameras along the alley. According to Roxanna, the place had an old security system that the occupants rarely bothered to set. This part of Glendale wasn't exactly a high crime area.

By the time I made it to the back entrance, Jackson was approaching from the opposite end of the alley. He pulled out his lockpicking tools, ready to get to work.

"Too late," I said with a smile, pulling out my own tools, then pushing the door open. It was a piece of cake.

Jackson nodded approvingly. "Let's see how you do on the safe."

Once we were both safely inside, we were greeted by a strong, musty scent, and dust-filled air that made both of us cough.

"They must not use this place too often," Jackson said. "If I can't breathe in this dungeon, there's no way Tony could. That man is a heart attack waiting to happen."

I pressed the back of my hand to my nose as I shined my flashlight around the small office. There were three cubicles in the middle of the floor, and an office on both the north and south sides of the building. Tony's was clearly marked in the far corner facing Glendale Boulevard. To our delight, the door wasn't even locked.

"I hope the rest of this caper is as easy as getting in here," Jackson said.

"Agreed."

We entered Tony's office, but as I moved to close the door, Jackson stopped me. "Leave it open. I highly doubt any of these old codgers will be interrupting us tonight. But if we do hear something and need to make a fast escape, that door's our only way out."

I glanced over at the large picture window. There was indeed no opening. If we ended up being cornered, we'd have to break through the window to escape.

The safe was located in a more than obvious location. Jackson removed a large, colorful painting of an elaborate chessboard to reveal the safe.

Just as Roxanna said, it was a high-tech electronic safe.

"How does she know all this stuff?" I said.

"Beats me. But she's damn good at what she does."

Pulling out the instructions Roxanna had given us with the code to the safe, I scanned the long sequence of numbers. We'd agreed that Jackson would enter the numbers, while I read them to him. There were thirty-seven digits in all. We only had three attempts. After that, the code would automatically reset and a new code would be instantly emailed to Tony, along with a notification of the failed attempts.

I pointed my flashlight at the card Roxanna had hand printed for us. Her writing was overly embellished, with unnecessary curlicues, even with numbers. I'd drawn a line after every five digits.

"Okay, let's get to it," Jackson said, positioning his flashlight so that it highlighted the keypad.

I began calling out the numbers. "Seven, two, five—"

"Slow down," Jackson snapped.

"Okay, okay. Just relax. We got this," I reassured him. I could tell he was nervous. I was too. But we'd already accomplished the hard part. We were in the building.

I called out the next five digits, much more slowly this time. When Jackson punched in the last number, nothing happened.

We looked at each other, our mutual surprise visible even in the near darkness.

"Are you sure you read the numbers correctly?" Jackson said, his tone critical.

"Of course I did."

"You aren't dyslexic, are you?"

I rolled my eyes. "No, I'm not dyslexic. Let's try it again. Just make sure you're entering them correctly."

"I entered the numbers exactly as you gave them to me. Aren't you watching me?"

"No, I'm not. I was trying to make sure I gave you the right numbers. But if you want me to do your job and mine, too, I can."

"Let me see that paper," he said, taking it from my hand before I could give it to him.

He studied it for several seconds, then handed it back to me.

"Okay, let's try it again."

I inhaled and began reading the numbers to him again, this time at an even slower pace. "Just three digits left," I said. "Two, nine, zero."

"Two, nine, zero," Jackson mumbled to himself as he entered the code.

Again, the safe didn't open.

"What's going on, Mac?" Jackson hissed.

"Maybe Roxanna gave us the wrong code," I said. "Nobody's perfect."

"No way. Roxanna knows her stuff." Jackson rubbed his forehead. "We only have one try left. Make sure you're reading the numbers correctly."

"You don't need to tell me that again. Don't blame me because it's not opening."

"Nobody's blaming you."

"Yes, you are. You just said—"

Jackson held up his right palm. "Look, we don't have time for your sensitivities right now. This is it. Our last attempt."

He took the card from me again and took several moments to study it.

"It's not like you can memorize it," I said. "I'm telling you I read the numbers correctly."

He continued to stare at the paper. "Hold up. You said the last three numbers were two, nine, zero. That's wrong. It's two, zero, nine."

"No, I am not." I snatched the card back and studied the numbers myself. "I read exactly what's on this paper. Two, zero, nine."

"No, you told me two, nine, zero."

I huffed. "No, I didn't."

"Yes, you did."

"Whatever."

"Just get it right," Jackson barked.

Once again, I carefully read the numbers out loud, while also checking to make sure he entered them correctly. When we got to the last two numbers, I paused to place emphasis on the last three digits. "Two . . . zero . . . nine."

I was about to hold my breath, but I didn't have time. We heard a click, followed by the door opening ever so slightly.

"Whew," Jackson said. "Hallelujah."

He opened the door wider to reveal just one item inside. He retrieved a sealed white letter-sized envelope with nothing written on it.

"That has to be Vincent's will," I said.

"I'm sure it is," Jackson said. "But the question is, will it tell us what we want to know?"

Jackson picked up a letter opener from Tony's desk and slid it into a corner of the envelope. He pulled out a document and started reading, using his flashlight.

"Well?" I asked anxiously. "Is that the will?"

Jackson didn't answer me. He just kept reading. "Naw," he said, clearly disappointed. "This first page is just a deed to a burial plot. Let me look at the other pages."

"Hurry," I said, trying to read over his shoulder. "We need to get out of here."

"Yes!" Jackson said, hoisting a fist in the air. "This is it."

"So what does it say?"

Before he could answer, we were startled by a loud, gruff voice.

"Hold it right there."

Chapter 33

JACKSON

That deep and methodical menacing voice slithering from the shadows behind us made me shudder, nearly causing me to drop the letter opener.

Not daring to turn, Mackenzie and I stood stock-still, our quickened breaths almost in sync. We both knew with grim certainty that the masked man had somehow found us again. And when bad guys utter demands like *Hold it right there*, odds are they're pointing a gun.

"Don't turn around," he said. "And don't say a word. Just listen."

The voice sounded almost too gruff, unnatural. He was clearly disguising his voice.

"I have a gun pointed at your backs," he continued, confirming the obvious. "So do exactly as you're told. You're going to pass that document to me. If it contains the information we're both looking for, I'll take it in exchange for your lives. But if I come up empty—I'll have to eliminate the competition."

"You're going to kill us?" Mackenzie blurted out. "Just like that?"

"Just take it," I said. "Take the will and—"

THWIP, THWIP!

Mackenzie and I flinched as silenced shots stung the wall beside the safe, throwing up puffs of drywall."

"Shut up!" the man snapped. "One more word and you're both dead."

Fear darkened Mackenzie's eyes and I was sure mine looked the same. We were helpless. Trapped.

"Mackenzie," the voice behind us said, "all you need to do is remain perfectly still. Understand?"

Mackenzie nodded stiffly. "Yes."

"Good girl," he said. "Now, Jackson, very slowly, and without turning around, I want you to reach back and hand me those papers. Do it now."

The fact that the man knew our names, while his identity remained a mystery to us, served as a chilling demonstration of how completely Mackenzie and I had been outplayed—a show of dominance that escalated my dread. Struggling to keep my hand steady, I carefully extended the document backward.

Soft, approaching footsteps behind us marred the silence before the envelope was snatched from my grasp, and then the footsteps quickly retreated.

He did exactly what I would've done: maintain distance. A firearm loses much of its advantage in close quarters.

"Let's see what we got," the darkness said, followed by the soft rustling of papers. Knowing that our lives depended on what was printed on those pages made even a common sound terrifying.

Then dozens of loose papers went flying, and fluttered to the floor at our feet.

Not a good sign at all.

I stopped breathing, while Mackenzie's breath quickened, almost panting.

"It's not here," the man said, his tone ominous. "Nothing personal, but I really have no choice."

Mackenzie's desperate eyes caught mine, then ever-so-slightly she jerked her head back in the man's direction and silently mouthed two words. I wasn't 100 percent sure I had read her lips correctly, but it looked like she said, *Distract him.* No time to second-guess, I spun around just in time to confirm that it was indeed the masked man and that his finger was tensing on the trigger.

"Wait," I said, throwing up my hands, "I think I just figured out the location of Keane's stash."

The masked man's trigger finger froze. Through the wide slit in his balaclava, his eyes narrowed skeptically, but there was also a flicker of interest.

"What are you talking about?" he barked, his gun now aimed at my head.

"I said—"

"I know what you just said. If you really know something, spit it out. Where is it?"

His focus, now riveted to me, gave Mackenzie just enough time to be brilliant. Her fingers flew to the safe's keypad, rapidly stabbing numbers.

A deafening emergency alarm began to scream and every light in the office turned on, full brightness.

"What the hell?" the masked man shouted as he opened fire.

THWIP, THWIP, THWIP, THWIP!

Bullets stinging around us, Mackenzie and I dove into a nearby cubicle. As more shots pierced the cubicle's padded wall, we both pulled our guns and fired back.

BAM, BAM, BAM, BAM!

The masked man dived behind a desk. He sprang up, fired a few more rounds, then melted into darkness as he sprinted out the open door. Gone.

My heart thrumming, I turned to Mackenzie and shouted over the still blaring alarm, "Are you okay?"

She nodded, panting. "I'm good, I'm good."

As we pulled ourselves to our feet, I asked, "How the hell did you do that?"

Mackenzie poked the safe's keypad again and the alarm went silent, then she replied, "The safe has a panic code. It was in the manual Roxanna gave us. Clearly you didn't read it."

"We already had the combo," I said in my defense. "Anyway, how the hell did you remember that code?"

"It's just 911 twice," Mackenzie said with a shrug. "Easy."

If I had any doubts about partnering up with maybe the stuffiest and quirkiest Black woman alive, those doubts dissolved at that moment. "You saved our lives," I said, then I pulled Mackenzie into my arms and gave her a big sloppy kiss.

When I finally let her go, she looked a little dazed and very much confused.

"That was just a thank-you kiss. That's all."

"Good to know," Mackenzie said. "And you're very welcome."

Then we just smiled at each other, almost certainly thinking the exact same thing.

It felt damn good to be alive.

Due to the sound of approaching police sirens we had to cut our little moment short.

Chapter 34

MACKENZIE

I don't think my heart can take another near-death experience," I said, once we were safely back inside Jackson's Benz and miles away from the murderous masked man.

When Jackson didn't respond, I just figured he was still grappling with his own trauma. So I left him to his thoughts. Neither of us uttered a word for the rest of the ride back to Inglewood. Jackson didn't even turn on any music.

"You okay?" I finally asked, as we were climbing out of his car back at my place.

"Nope. I'm anything but fine. Something's not right."

"What do you mean?"

"That guy knows our every move. Prentice knew nothing about the safe, so there's no way Bioff or Meza or their henchman could've known about it either. The only way someone could've tracked us to that office was by spying on us."

"Spying on us? How?"

He shrugged. "How would *you* spy on someone?"

Suddenly, a lightbulb went off in my head. "You think he put a tracker on your car?"

"I wouldn't doubt it," Jackson said.

We both pulled out our flashlights and began scouring every inch of Jackson's Benz, looking for the tracker. We checked the car's underbody, the wheels, the tires, the front and back bumpers, as well as the hood and trunk. Then Jackson told me to recheck the areas he had searched, while he double-checked the places I had searched.

"There's nothing here," I said.

"Let's check the inside, too," Jackson said.

We took our time, practically dismantling his Benz. We searched the glove compartment, underneath the dashboard, the visors, the seats and the carpets, in between the seats, and even the ceiling. Jackson even took a tool from his trunk so he could lift the back and front seats.

"Nothing," he said, angrily throwing the tool back into the trunk. "But I'm not crazy. There's no other explanation for this guy knowing our every move."

"I agree," I said. "But the tracking devices they make these days are so small, it could be impossible to find."

Jackson leaned back against the car and massaged his eyes with his thumb and index fingers.

"If he didn't plant a tracking device on the car," he said wearily, "maybe he installed a listening device in your town house. The only time we talked about breaking into Tony's office was in my car when we were leaving the park and at your place last night."

The mere thought that the wannabe killer had possibly invaded my personal space made me shiver with fear. Without another word, we both rushed inside and did an equally thorough search of every inch of my town house.

Once again, our search came up empty. By the time we were done nearly thirty minutes later, I was as exhausted as I was frustrated. We both slumped onto my living room couch.

"That guy's not some phantom ghost," Jackson said. "There's no way he can know our every move without following us or knowing in advance where we're going."

"I'm pretty sure he didn't follow us to Glendale. My neck is still sore from constantly looking around as you were driving. He—"

Jackson jumped to his feet.

"What's wrong?" I said.

He placed a finger to his lips, then held up his cell phone in one hand and pointed to it with the other.

"You think—"

This time Jackson vertically swiped his hand across his neck, mimicking a throat-slitting gesture.

He frantically looked around the room, then grabbed a small notepad and pen from my kitchen counter. With rapid strokes, he scribbled a note, tore the page from the pad, and thrust it at me.

It's probably our phones.

I nodded my agreement. But how could someone hack our phones when they were always in our possession?

Jackson started writing again, then tossed me another page from the notepad.

Turn off your phone.

I did as he instructed.

"This is crazy. I can't believe—"

This time Jackson hushed me by repeating the throat-cutting signal with both of his hands.

I was totally confused. If our phones were somehow tapped and we had just turned them off, why weren't we free to talk?

Grabbing the notepad, I wrote him a message.

Why can't we talk if the phones are off?

I handed the notepad back to him and waited for his response.

Because turning off our phones may not be enough.

Chapter 35

JACKSON

The following morning, as Mackenzie and I sped back to Roxanna's place in my Mercedes, we talked about anything and everything except our actual destination. If, as we suspected, the masked man had somehow tapped our phones or installed a tracker on the car, we didn't want him showing up at Roxy's place, guns blazing.

When Mac and I ran out of things to small-talk about, I cranked up the Benz's premium sound system and filled the car with my old-school R&B playlist. Legends like Aretha Franklin, the Temptations, and of course Smokey had us bobbing our heads as we cruised through Crenshaw and the Wilshire district—like we didn't have a worry in the world. Al Green's smooth, soulful voice was crooning "Let's Stay Together," my mom's favorite song, when we finally wheeled into Roxanna's driveway.

Unaccustomed to us showing up without notice, when Roxanna opened her door and saw her two favorite PIs on her doorstep, she looked absolutely stunned. Before Roxanna could ask any questions, I urgently shook my head and pressed a finger to my lips.

Don't speak.

Simultaneously, Mackenzie held up a sheet of paper bearing the handwritten message—*our phones might be tapped.*

Roxanna's eyes widened with understanding, and without uttering a word, she beckoned us inside. Moments later, we were in an ultra-high-tech home office, worthy of Batman, watching over Roxanna's shoulder as she scrutinized scrolling data on multiple monitors. Both Mackenzie's cell phone and mine were connected to a fat, glowing computer tower by USB cables. The data that held Roxanna riveted was being fed directly from our devices.

Roxanna's surprised expressions and body language told us that whatever she saw in that code impressed the hell out of her. Then she began typing. Her fingers flew over the keyboard with impossible speed, the staccato click of keys as rapid as machine gunfire. On the monitors, long strings of new code raced across the screen, line after line, almost faster than the eye could follow. Then, abruptly, she stopped.

Roxanna raised her hands from the keyboard like a concert pianist completing a recital.

"I am done," she declared. "Your phones have been restored to normal."

"Then we were right," I said. "They were tapped."

Roxanna shook her head. "No, this word *tapped*, it is too simplistic. A forwarding routine was injected into the kernel-level code of your phones—and somehow all done remotely. This is not a tap; it is telephony wizardry. The person who did this even scares me."

"Wait," Mackenzie said. "Are you saying the masked man's hacking skills are as good as yours?"

"No," Roxanna said. "It is nearly impossible your masked man did this hack himself. Anyone with this level of skill would not bother running around trying to kill people. More likely he had help. Very expensive help."

"Like the kind of help a major crime organization could afford," I said.

"This is correct," Roxanna said, then she disconnected our cell phones from her computer. Instead of handing them back, she held the devices before us and explained, "I have added a snippet of code to your devices that will stop a repeat attack. But, like I said, these people after you are very good—meaning they are very, very bad. There are other ways they can get to you. Do you understand this?"

Mackenzie and I nodded solemnly, then reached for our phones, but Roxanna snatched them back out of our reach. Pinning us both with tough-love eyes, she said, "If you two get yourselves killed, I will be very sad, yes—but I will never forgive you. Never."

Then Roxanna handed back our phones.

Instead of instilling fear in us, the revelation that our personal cell phones had been hacked sparked outrage. Enough was enough.

It was time to confront Prentice and let the chips fall where they may.

Chapter 36

MACKENZIE

As we sat in the lobby of Willis Worldwide, Jackson's left leg kept bouncing up and down. His jaw was stretched tight and he stared straight ahead. At the moment, I was a lot more worried about what Jackson would say to Prentice than what Prentice would say to us.

"So, exactly what do you plan to tell Prentice?" I asked, desperately wanting a preview of Jackson's impending explosion. I'd never seen him this angry before.

"I have no idea," Jackson said.

"Well, why don't you let me take the lead?"

He turned to look at me. "I got this."

"I know you do, but you're clearly upset. I'm upset too. But don't forget that these guys are deadly killers. Just don't go in there making threats we can't back up."

"I'll do whatever I—"

The receptionist interrupted us to escort us to Prentice's office. Jackson jumped ahead of her, stalking down the impressive hallway.

When she showed us inside, Prentice was sitting on his couch with a white cloth napkin tucked into the collar of his pristine white shirt, enjoying a huge plate of shrimp cocktail and a bottle of champagne.

"How are my two favorite private investigators?" he said with a smile, raising his glass to us. "Are you here with some good news? You're quite welcome to join me for an afternoon snack."

"Your two favorite investigators," Jackson said, his voice laced with sarcasm, "are tired of all the bullshit. As we told you days ago, someone's trying to kill us. What have you done to find out whether one of your cohorts is behind the attacks on us?"

The smile briefly left Prentice's face, then quickly reappeared.

"I don't like your tone," Prentice said, looking up at us. "You need to check yourself. Why don't you have a seat and enjoy some of these delicious Argentinian red shrimp prepared by my personal chef?"

"I don't need to check myself. And I don't want a seat or any of your fucking shrimp."

I gently placed a hand on Jackson's forearm. "Why don't you let me take it from here," I said.

Jackson pinned me with a gaze hot enough to burn a hole through my forehead. "I already told you I got this," he said through clenched teeth.

"Since you don't seem to understand the urgency of our request," Jackson said, turning back to Prentice, "I'd like to speak to your father. Is he here?"

Prentice chuckled arrogantly, then stuffed a whole shrimp in his mouth and took his time chewing it.

"My father asked me to handle this matter," Prentice said, talking with his mouth full. "So you talk to me and only me."

"Not anymore," Jackson insisted. "You've done absolutely nothing to find out who's trying to kill us. That's not acceptable. We either talk to your father or we're out."

Prentice removed the napkin from his chest and slowly rose to his feet. He was a head taller than Jackson, who stubbornly continued to stand his ground.

"Lucky for you I'm a reasonable man," Prentice began, staring down at Jackson. "I understand that you're under a great deal of pressure right now, but that comes with the territory. So I guess you'll just need to toughen up a bit. But understand this," he paused for several long beats, "I don't appreciate you coming onto my turf disrespecting me. Don't let it happen again."

"Nobody's disrespecting you," Jackson said, refusing to cower. "We're just not willing to put our lives on the line for this job."

Prentice shrugged. "In another twenty-four hours, it won't matter what you do."

I stepped forward. "What does that mean?"

"I guess you haven't heard," Prentice said. "Vincent Keane died in the hospital this morning."

I gasped. "I thought he was getting better."

"That's what we thought as well, but he suddenly took a turn for the worse. Now that he's dead, it won't be long before that information is released to the police."

Jackson and I silently contemplated the significance of Keane's death for Big Ced and the other two crime bosses. If the information Keane was holding over their heads was as devastating as they assumed it was, all three men would surely go to prison.

Jackson looked at me, then grinned and started brushing his palms back and forth. "Then I guess we're done. Sorry we couldn't help you." He turned to leave.

"Not so fast," Prentice said, stopping him. "The way I see it, you now have less than twenty-four hours to find the evidence before the police get their hands on it. So now the *real* clock is ticking."

"You have to be kidding me," Jackson said. "We don't have any other leads."

"Then find some," Prentice demanded. "If that information gets out and my father and the other two men go down, I promise what happens to you will be much worse."

Chapter 37

JACKSON

Mackenzie and I beelined to our new Culver City office, where we sat behind our temporary desks, lunching on passable take-out pizza while trying to decide our next move. Instead of manning the reception desk, like we paid her to do, Nadine had dragged over a folding chair to offer up her two cents. To be honest, the heat was really cranked up now and I wasn't in the mood to give PI lessons to my cousin—but I also didn't want to waste time, so I decided to keep the peace and keep it moving.

We were each two slices deep and had yet to come up with anything more promising than what appeared to be our only remaining option. Earlier, when I told Prentice that we were all out of leads, I wasn't being honest. Mackenzie and I still hadn't dragged our asses out to Bakersfield to sit down with Rebecca Keane. Considering what we were hunting for, Vincent Keane's only child, no matter how far away she lived, should've been our first stop. However, father and daughter hadn't spoken in over a decade, which in my mind greatly diminished the likelihood that Keane would've trusted her with something so important. For this reason, although Mackenzie and her new trainee, Nadine, were already set on Bakersfield, I was still trying to think outside the pizza box. But, after looking at the case from all angles, there seemed to be no other move left.

Just as I was about to concede to the ladies and shift our focus to planning an early morning drive out to the desert, we heard someone knocking at the front entrance. The door separating Mackenzie's and my shared back office from the reception area was shut, so we had no clue who our visitor might be.

"Oh shit," Nadine said, her mouth half full of pizza, "I wonder who that could be."

"Here's an idea," I said to her. "Why don't you get up and go investigate?"

"Are you serious?" Nadine said. "How do you know it's not that crazy killer in the mask?"

"Elementary, my dear," I said, affecting my best British accent. "I seriously doubt a masked murderer would knock on our door in the middle of the day." Then I turned to Mackenzie. "Wouldn't you concur, Watson?"

Mackenzie rolled her eyes, then said to Nadine, "Your cousin's a little weird—but he's also right. You'll be fine."

Nadine shrugged. "Okay, if you say so." She dropped her pizza, wiped her mouth with a napkin, and went to answer the door.

Mackenzie frowned and shook her head at me. "Your Sherlock Holmes impression sucks."

"It's way better when I'm wearing the goofy hat," I said.

"I seriously doubt it."

Nadine reappeared in the office doorway. "You were right," she said. "It's not a killer. It's a police detective. He says he needs to talk to you two."

"Let me guess," I said. "He's tall, almost as well dressed as me, and smells like the first floor of Macy's."

"You left out sexy," Nadine said. "I need me a man like that."

"Careful," I said. "You're talking about Mackenzie's boyfriend."

Nadine's wide eyes shot to Mackenzie. "Seriously?"

"Don't listen to Jackson," Mackenzie said. "The lieutenant and I went on one date. That's it."

"Annnd?" Nadine said.

"Annnd—would you send the man in already?" Mackenzie said.

"Yeah, and you stay out there," I also said to Nadine. "It's for your own good."

"Whatever," she muttered, as she disappeared through the door.

An instant later Lieutenant Gooden strode into our office looking like he'd just left a GQ photo shoot. He flashed a perfect smile at Mackenzie. "Hey, Macky. Good to see you again."

"Good to see you, too, Mark," Mackenzie replied with a smile.

"Macky?" I said, doing a double take. "Who the hell is Macky?"

Lieutenant Gooden chuckled. "Good to see you, too, Jackson. In fact, to be quite honest, I'm glad to see that you two are still alive. Considering."

"Considering what exactly?" I said.

Ignoring my question, he glanced around our office while nodding appreciatively. "Hey, this is a nice little setup. Some snazzier decor and this place could really be something."

I couldn't believe my ears. For a few seconds my raw dislike for the man ticked down a few notches. I said to Mackenzie, "You hear that, Macky? When it comes to office decor this man knows what he's talking about."

"Would you hush?" Mackenzie turned to Gooden. "So, what can we do for you?"

"Actually, I'm here to do something for you two," he said. "I have information to share. Vincent Keane is dead. Never woke up from the coma."

Of course, Mackenzie and I already knew this, courtesy of Prentice, but we couldn't let Gooden know that. As if we'd rehearsed for this very moment, Mackenzie and I simultaneously reacted with a mix of remorse and puzzlement.

"That's awful, Mark," Mackenzie said. "But why would you come here to tell us that in person?"

"In other words," I said, "why would we care?"

"Good question," Gooden said, "Because we both know that you do care. Keane's key to whatever you two are mixed up in. Now that he's out of the picture I was hoping I'd get some cooperation. I was hoping that you'd tell me how Keane is connected to Big Ced, Meza, and Bioff. Well?"

I splayed my palms. "Sorry, but we really don't know anything."

Lieutenant Gooden turned to Mackenzie. "You too? You're going to continue this game?"

"It's not a game, Mark," Mackenzie said. "If we knew something we'd—"

Lieutenant Gooden raised a hand. "Forget it. I'm done." He sighed. "I guess whatever the connection is, Vincent Keane will take that secret to his grave."

Holy shit!

I sat up in my chair. Gooden's words struck me like a light turning on in a pitch-black room. Suddenly it was all clear.

I glanced over at Mackenzie and she, too, was sitting upright, eyes wide, equally thunderstruck, hopefully, by the same realization.

"Are you two all right?" Lieutenant Gooden asked. "You both look kind of—"

"Oh no," I interrupted, glancing at my watch. "Mac, we got that one twenty urgent appointment coming in. Remember?"

Mackenzie snapped her fingers. "You're right." She frowned at

Lieutenant Gooden. "Mark, we're going to have to ask you to leave. Like, right now. Sorry."

"Sure. No problem," the detective said, his brow furrowed. "But before I go, are you busy tonight?"

Mackenzie winced. "Damn, actually I'm tied up. Let's do it another night, okay?"

"Definitely looking forward to it," he said, giving Mackenzie a suave smile. Then, as he headed for the door, he added, "You two be careful. I mean that. Goodbye."

The instant Lieutenant Gooden walked out, Mackenzie practically leaped across the office and locked the door behind him. Unable to contain our excitement a second longer, the answer we had searched so hard for burst from our mouths at the same instant. "The burial plot!"

Lieutenant Gooden's remark about Keane taking a secret to his grave had triggered a shared memory. Back in Bonaducchi's office, the envelope that contained Keane's will—also held the deed to a burial plot.

Mackenzie and I began pacing as we methodically broke down our theory. Not only were we on the same page, it was as if we were thinking with the same mind.

"Think about it," I said. "What better place to hide something you want found only after your death than a bought-and-paid-for gravesite?"

"Exactly," Mackenzie said. "And what's brilliant is that this method doesn't rely on someone else to follow your posthumous instructions."

"Yup. Doing it this way is literally foolproof."

"No one's going to touch that patch of earth until it's time to dig your grave," Mackenzie said.

"And when the gravediggers start shoveling," I said, "guess what they're going to find."

"Definitely some kind of moisture-proof container," Mackenzie said. "Airtight, even."

"Bingo. Can't have mold or worms ruining files that can topple three criminal empires."

Mackenzie shook her head. "Nope. Can't have that."

Then we stopped pacing and for a lingering moment just stared at each other—both hesitant to voice the obvious unspoken question.

Mackenzie broke the silence. "This is it, isn't it?"

"Sure feels like it," I said. "I mean, this has to be it. But we won't know for sure until we dig it up."

"Yuck, but yeah."

I grimaced. "Yuck is right. I don't have anything to wear to a grave-robbing."

Mackenzie gasped and grabbed my arm. "Jackson, I just thought of something. After someone passes, how soon does the cemetery start preparing the grave?"

I instantly understood my partner's urgent tone. If anyone dug up that grave before we did, very soon someone might be digging graves for the two of us. I said to Mackenzie, "I'd imagine it usually takes a few days at least, but we're not taking any chances. We're digging up that plot tonight."

"Tonight, tonight?"

"Damn skippy."

I quickly got Roxanna on the phone and within ten minutes she had emailed us all the information we needed: the name of the cemetery, the plot number, and an up-to-date burial plot map.

After reviewing the information, Mackenzie said to me, "You do realize that Westwood Village Memorial Park is one of the most expensive cemeteries in the entire world, right?"

"I actually do know that."

"Expensive means exclusive, which means lots of security."

I nodded. "Of course. Makes sense."

Mackenzie crossed her arms. "Jackson Jones, how in hell do you expect us to break into a secure cemetery with zero planning?"

"If I could answer that," I said, "then that would actually be a plan, wouldn't it, Macky?"

"Don't call me that again—and we're going to need shovels."

"Good thinking. See—now we got ourselves a plan."

Chapter 38

MACKENZIE

I thought Jackson was joking when he said he'd never been to a Home Depot, but as we combed the aisles, the sheer awe in his eyes told me it was true.

"This place is huge," Jackson said, looking around. "This is like a giant toy store for handymen."

We were there to pick up two shovels for our upcoming cemetery expedition, a task that still made me uneasy.

"How is it possible that you've never been to a Home Depot?" I asked him. "Don't you ever have repairs at your place?"

"Sure, but I never fix stuff myself. I hire people for that." He paused in front of a display of kitchen tiles. "Wow. I can't believe how many different tiles they have. There's some hella nice stuff in here. Who knew?"

"You're unbelievable," I said, annoyed. "The shovels should be in the back near the gardening section. Follow me."

We made our way there and were confronted with so many different kinds of shovels it was almost overwhelming.

"I would ask you which one we should get," I said, "but I suspect you have no idea."

"And you would be right. I don't do manual labor if I can help it."

I opened the Home Depot app on my phone and started reading the descriptions of the various shovels. "This forty-three-inch carbon-steel digging shovel has some pretty good reviews," I said.

Jackson took my phone. "Let me see that. Who would take the time to write a review for a friggin' shovel?"

"People who care about gardening," I said, taking my phone back. "This one has over four stars. People describe it as *light, strong, and great*. That's good enough for me."

I reached for two of them.

"Hold up. Those look cheap. This one has a fiberglass handle."

I took hold of it. "It's also twice as heavy and costs three times as much. It won't work. Let's go."

Jackson grudgingly followed me to the self-checkout line.

"I don't do self-checkout," he said, frowning. "If I'm spending my money, I want some personal service."

I could only shake my head.

"Aw, that's cute," he said, when I pulled out my credit card. "You actually have an orange Home Depot card. I only use American Express. Platinum, of course."

"Of course." I grabbed the receipt. "Why are you in such a jovial mood? We could be hours away from death."

"It is what it is," Jackson said. "But I have a good feeling about this."

The drive to Westwood Village Memorial Park took us about forty minutes. I was driving my Jeep because Jackson insisted he didn't want to risk getting any dirt in his Benz.

When I saw the high steel gates and concrete slabs surrounding the huge cemetery, I pulled over to the curb across the street and parked.

"How in the hell are we going to get in there?" I asked. "That place looks like a fortress."

"With this." Jackson pulled a wad of fifty-dollar bills from his pocket.

"What makes you think you'll be able to bribe someone?"

"There are a ton of celebrities buried in there," Jackson said, excitedly. "Marilyn Monroe, Dean Martin, Truman Capote, Kirk Douglas, just to name a few."

"I would love to know how you know that, but I'm afraid to ask."

"I'm a big movie buff."

"Okay," I said, stretching out the word. "I still don't get the bribe connection. How is the fact that celebrities are buried in there going to get us inside when the place is clearly closed?"

"I'll bet you anything the guards are used to people sneaking in. We're going to tell them we want to see Marilyn Monroe's grave and flash my cash."

"I have no desire to see Marilyn Monroe's grave or anyone else's."

"Just drive over there and follow my lead."

We pulled up to the huge steel gates and rolled to stop. A security guard walked over to greet us.

"I'm sorry, ma'am, but we're closed."

"I can't believe we didn't make it here in time," Jackson said with a sophisticated British accent. He leaned over to make eye contact with the guard. "The traffic here is abysmal. I'm visiting all the way from London. I wanted to get a picture of Marilyn Monroe's gravesite. It's on my bucket list."

"I'm sorry, sir. You're free to come back in the morning. We open at ten."

"But my plane leaves early tomorrow. Could I offer you a little incentive to let us run over there and take a quick picture?" Jackson flashed the thick roll of cash. "We'll be in and out in seconds."

The guy actually licked his lips as he eyed the cash.

"I promise we'll make it quick," Jackson pressed.

The guy nervously looked around, then stuck out his hand. Jackson filled it with the wad of cash.

"If another guard or one of the groundskeepers catches you, you're on your own."

"Tell me I'm amazing," Jackson said, as we drove past the gates.

"Yeah, whatever. Pull out that map and direct me to Vincent's plot."

The sprawling cemetery was the size of a few football fields. Without the map from Roxanna, we would've been searching for Vincent's plot for days. But we found it relatively fast.

"Let's hurry," I said, hopping out and grabbing the shovels.

We immediately started digging. Surprisingly, the dirt wasn't very firmly packed, which made the digging a lot easier. That also made me think something had recently been buried here. We'd dug about two feet down before we needed to take a short break to catch our breaths. We dug another foot or so; still nothing.

"It isn't here," I said, pausing to lean on my shovel for another rest break.

"Yes, it is," Jackson said, continuing to dig. "It has to be."

I watched him dig as Prentice's threat replayed in my mind. *If that information gets out and my father and the other two men go down, I promise you'll be going down with them.*

Suddenly, I heard a clink.

"I hit something," Jackson said excitedly.

He started digging more vigorously, and I joined in.

"This is it," Jackson said, shining his flashlight down into the hole.

We clearly saw a metal container with a padlock on it. It was about four times the size of a lunch box. Jackson squatted down and tugged it free.

For the next few seconds, we were so choked up with emotion, we couldn't speak.

Jackson set the box back on the ground, then started pounding the padlock with his shovel.

"Jackson, stop! What're you doing?"

"I'm opening it."

"No way," I said. "We don't want to see that information. If we give them an open box, they'll know we read it."

"We can buy another lock to put on it," Jackson said. "We have to be sure. I won't read the information."

"No!" I insisted.

Jackson ignored me and kept slamming the lock with the shovel until it finally fell off.

"Shine your flashlight on it," Jackson said as he opened the box.

Inside, we discovered three small notebooks, each bearing the name of one of the crime bosses. There was also a short cover letter instructing that the binders be delivered to the police upon Vincent's death.

Jackson looked at me. He was still breathing heavily from the workout.

"We did it," he said, his voice cracking. "We found it. Now let's get the hell out of here."

Chapter 39

JACKSON

We decided to hold off on reporting our discovery until we were safely back at Mackenzie's town house. Only after Mac and I were settled on her sofa, drinks in hand, with the metal box on the coffee table before us, did I speed dial Big Ced's son. When Prentice's recorded voice answered, I wanted to hurl my iPhone across the living room. Instead, I left a brief voicemail urging him to call us back tonight. ASAP.

With nothing left to do but wait, Mackenzie sipped her wine, I sipped my scotch, and we both stared at that metal box as if it were a treasure chest. On our way home we stopped at a Target to replace the padlock. For some reason we wasted time trying to find one similar to the original lock—although it really didn't matter, no one had seen it but us and a dead man.

"Aren't you curious?" I asked Mackenzie.

"About what?"

"About what's in those three notebooks?"

"Of course," she said. "But sometimes it's better not knowing."

I wagged a finger at her. "Right—like why Lieutenant Good-teeth has his very own sweetheart nickname for you."

Mackenzie nodded. "Exactly. Also, like why a supposedly sophisticated Black man who has lived his whole damn life in Los Angeles has never heard of the architect Paul Williams?"

I stifled a gasp. How the hell could she know that? Nah, no way, she had to be fishing. I laughed it off and said, "What are you talking about? Back in the day, Paul Revere Williams designed some of the most iconic buildings in SoCal. He also designed, like, dozens of celebrity homes. So many that they called him *Hollywood's Architect*. See, I know all about the man."

After a smirk and a slow sip of wine Mackenzie said, "I'll give you points for looking him up. The only reason I didn't call you out in front of Roxanna is because I didn't want to embarrass you."

"But—"

"But if you keep trying to deny it," Mackenzie barreled on, "I'll make it a point to tell Roxy. And maybe I'll tell Nicole too." Mackenzie pinned me with dead certain eyes. "You know I'm right—just admit it."

"Fine," I said with a sigh.

While Mackenzie chuckled, I took a big gulp of scotch.

I was about to ask Miss Know-it-all how she'd managed to see through me, when my phone rang and Prentice's name flashed onscreen. I answered, and before he could utter a single word, I explained our recent phone hack issue and the possibility that his phone might also be compromised. Understanding my caution, Prentice agreed to call back from a safe phone in a few minutes.

True to his word, less than five minutes later my phone rang again, and I put it on speaker.

Prentice's deep voice filled the living room. "Okay, we should be good. What's going on? I hope it's good news."

"It's very good news," I said. "We did it. We found Keane's files."

"This legit? Do not fuck with me."

"Nobody's fucking with you. Yes, this is legit."

"Yes!" he exclaimed. "Tell me—who had it?"

"Well, no one actually had it, per se."

"What the hell does that mean?"

"It's a little—complicated," I said.

"Complicated how?"

Mackenzie jumped in and quickly explained Keane's burial-plot ploy.

"That's not complicated," Prentice said. "That's damn genius."

"Agreed," Mackenzie and I replied in chorus.

"How do you know there's files in that metal box?" Prentice asked. "Did you two open it and look inside?"

Mackenzie shook her head at me unnecessarily because there was no way I was going to tell him we opened that box.

"No, sir," I said. "Like Mackenzie explained, the box is padlocked. But think about it. Keane went through a lot of trouble. What else would he hide in that hole?"

"That makes sense," Prentice said. "Okay, let's meet in an hour so I can take delivery."

Mackenzie silently shook her head at me again. This time I responded with a stiff nod, acknowledging what we both knew had to come next.

I took a steadying breath, then said to Prentice, "Sorry, but we can't make delivery to you."

"Excuse me? Why the hell not?"

Since day one of this case, Mackenzie and I decided that if and when we did find Keane's poison files, to be safe as well as professional, the handoff had to be done very carefully.

"No offense," I said to Prentice. "Technically we don't work for you. Meza, Bioff, and your father are the clients. For that reason, we can only deliver the files to them. In person. We hope you understand."

There was no reply.

For a long tense moment, the phone went silent.

Mackenzie and I just stared at each other and the phone, waiting.

When Prentice finally spoke again, surprisingly, there was no impatience or irritation in his voice. Instead, his tone was flat and almost too calm. "Okay, we'll do it your way. I'll arrange the meeting for tomorrow. You'll have the details first thing in the morning. Does this work for you?"

"Yes," I said. "Sounds perfect."

"Thank you for understanding," Mackenzie added.

"Of course. Good job, you two. Congratulations."

We both thanked him, and I was about to end the call when Prentice said, "One last thing. And this is very important." Then his voice dropped, and each deliberate word seemed to carry its own threat. "Guard that box like your lives depend on it. Because they do."

Then the call went dead, leaving a chill in its wake.

It took a moment for Mackenzie and me to shake off the weight of his words before raising our glasses for a toast.

"To getting paid big," I said.

"And to being alive to spend it," Mackenzie added with a smirk.

We clinked glasses and drained our drinks, then Mackenzie yawned and said, "I'm ready for a shower and bed. How about you?"

Any other night, an easy setup like that would pretty much demand I reply with a sexually charged joke. No way I'd be able to resist. But all that damn digging and refilling of that grave had taken its toll on a brother. It took energy to flirt with Mackenzie, and I had nothing left. At that moment a shower and sleep were all I needed.

"Sounds good to me," I said, then I nodded toward the metal box. "We can't just leave that there. Got someplace we can stash that?"

Mackenzie rose from the sofa and grabbed the box by its handle. "You go shower first, while I find someplace to put this thing."

"Okay." Then as I stood up, I said, "You're not just going to stick that in a closet, right?"

"Don't worry," Mackenzie said. "I got this."

• • •

I was awakened by Mackenzie nudging me and calling my name. She was sitting up in bed, her eyes edged with fear.

It was still dark outside. The bedside clock glowed 3:13 a.m. Assuming she'd had a bad dream, I sat up beside her and asked, "You okay?"

She shushed me, and only then did I notice that she was staring across the dark bedroom at the cracked-open door. "Listen," she whispered. "I think there's someone in the house."

My body tensed. "Are you sure?"

She shook her head and pressed a finger to her lips. "Just listen."

My ears pricked up.

Somewhere a dog barked, a car cruised down the street, and what sounded like the creak of footsteps.

I fished my gun from the bedside table drawer and sprang out of bed. "You wait here."

"Yeah, right." Mackenzie was already armed and on her feet, moving for the bedroom door.

Me wearing sweatpants and a T-shirt, and Mackenzie in pink flannel pajamas, we crept barefoot side by side down the hallway, our guns held ready.

We both froze, too stunned to move.

Either a soundless tornado had struck while we'd slept, or Mackenzie's living room had been searched.

Sofa pillows were tossed, wall unit doors hung wide open, the contents of the coat closet and another storage closet were strewn on the floor.

My heart racing, I said to Mackenzie, "Please tell me you hid that box well."

"Come on," Mackenzie said, rushing through the mess in the living room and leading me into the kitchen. Every cabinet door was open. Even the dishwasher and refrigerator had been searched. But far worse—I did not like the way Mackenzie stood there gaping into the open pantry. Her wide eyes riveted to a very empty shelf.

"It's gone," Mackenzie murmured. "Jackson, it's gone."

"You hid the box in there?" I snapped. "I specifically told you not to stick it in a closet."

"This isn't a closet," she said. "It's a pantry."

"Are you serious right now? A pantry is a closet!"

"Stop yelling at me!"

Our burgeoning shouting match was thankfully interrupted by the roar of a starting engine.

Mackenzie and I charged to the front door and threw it open in time to see the taillights of a black sedan tearing past her town house.

"I am so tired of that masked asshole," I said. "Come on."

Barely dressed, nothing on our feet, guns in our hands, we exploded from Mackenzie's place and raced to my car. The welcome jolt of crisp night air served to sharpen my senses.

"You really think we can catch him?" Mackenzie asked.

"We have to."

Chapter 40

MACKENZIE

Jackson's Benz raced down the street at breakneck speed, trailing after the only other car in sight. I prayed the taillights we saw blocks ahead of us belonged to the burglar who'd ransacked my place and boldly stolen the lockbox.

"Hey!" I yelled when Jackson blew through a red light without even slowing down to check for cross traffic. "You're going to get us killed."

"If we don't get that box back, we're dead anyway. So pick your poison."

Jackson's hands gripped the steering wheel at the ten-and-two position. His body leaned forward slightly as he was laser-focused on trying to catch the car ahead of us.

When the car made a sudden right turn and Jackson followed, I reached up for the grab handle and held on tight to keep from banging my head into the passenger window.

Jackson was closing the distance between us and what looked like an Escalade. His Benz was much faster than the gas-guzzling SUV the thief was driving. The fact that it was just after three in the morning was a big help because the streets were practically deserted. Only a single block separated us now.

The Escalade made another sharp turn onto a side street just past Florence Boulevard. Jackson continued flooring the Benz, the sound of the engine roaring. Now only about three car lengths separated us. Jackson accelerated again, ready to slam into the Escalade's rear end, when the driver made another unexpected move.

Just as we came upon a park, the SUV started doing donuts in the middle of the intersection.

"He must've lost control of the car," Jackson yelled.

Before we could figure out what was happening, the Escalade headed straight for us at top speed. A split second before it T-boned into the driver's side of Jackson's Benz, he jerked the steering wheel to the right, allowing us to escape the impact. The sharp move sent my head slamming into the window. We watched as the SUV plummeted into a thick telephone pole.

The driver jumped out of the Escalade and charged toward us. It was indeed the masked man. Just as he was about to reach the car, Jackson threw open the door, knocking him to the ground. As I climbed out and rounded Jackson's Benz, the man hopped to his feet, raised a gun, and fired at Jackson's head. The gunshot rang out at the same time I swung my leg in a well-timed Krav Maga move, kicking the gun from his hand.

Now weaponless, the man barreled forward, hurling his body into Jackson's chest, pounding his back against the trunk of the Mercedes.

Jackson's head banged into the car and he yelped in pain. Still, he somehow managed to reach out and snatch off the man's mask.

"What the hell?" Jackson said, as the man just stood there, seemingly dazed and out of breath.

I was standing behind him and didn't know what Jackson had

seen beneath the mask until the man turned around and charged toward me.

Another Krav Maga kick to the head and a punch to the man's nose sent him crumbling to his knees, wobbling from side to side.

Now I understood what Jackson had seen. Beneath the man's balaclava mask, his face was concealed by yet another mask. A hyper-realistic latex mask of a bald white man, so lifelike that in most situations it would fool anyone. But, because of the blows landed to the attacker's head, the latex mask had been partially dislodged. Through the now offset eyeholes, I could see that he wasn't white.

I reached down and snatched off the mask. Now I was the one in shock.

The man wasn't just Black, he was someone we knew. The man on his knees before us was Prentice Willis.

"You've been the one trying to kill us?" Jackson barked.

Prentice wiped his bloody nose with the back of his hand and sneered up at us.

"It wasn't supposed to go down like this."

"So how was it supposed to go down?" I asked. "Were we supposed to be dead by now?"

"No," Prentice said, actually smiling. "You two weren't going to die until *after* you retrieved the evidence. I should've killed you earlier tonight while you were asleep."

"Why didn't you just wait for us to bring you the lockbox," I said. "Why'd you have to steal it?"

"Because if my father got his hands on whatever is in that box, he would destroy it. That's not what I wanted to happen."

"What are you talking about?" Jackson said.

"I'm the one who should be running Willis Worldwide. He's a relic. The crime families should be working together, not protecting their turf and fighting each other. We can make way more money as a united front. It's time for change. But my father refuses to see things my way."

"So you were going to hand over the evidence to the police?" I asked. "To bring your father down?"

"Damn straight. And I still plan to."

In one fluid motion, Prentice reached toward his ankle, pulled out another gun, and aimed it up at me. Before I could react, his head exploded.

At that moment, I froze as Jackson stood across from me, his gun still extended as Prentice's body tumbled sideways to the ground.

I'm not sure how long we stood there, staring at Prentice's lifeless body. The distant sound of sirens eventually broke us out of our daze.

"We have to grab that lockbox and get out of here!" Jackson yelled, as he dashed toward Prentice's Escalade.

"We can't run," I said. "You just blew a man's head off!"

Jackson ignored me as he snatched the lockbox from the front seat of the Escalade and started toward his Benz.

"C'mon," he shouted, opening the door. "Let's go."

"No! If the police stop us and find that box, we're dead."

"We're already dead," Jackson fired back. "I killed Big Ced's only son."

I spun around, my eyes darting across the park in near darkness. Tall streetlamps cast elongated shadows, offering only a partial view of the park's grounds.

"Let's hide the lockbox and come back for it later." I pointed across the park. "Over there. We can stuff it behind those trash bins."

Jackson followed my gaze, then took off running as I chased after him.

When we reached the bins, Jackson wedged the lockbox between one of the bins and a brick wall. The space was so tight, it didn't even fall to the ground.

"Okay," I said, "we have to go back and wait for the police. What you did was self-defense. There must be some cameras around here to support that."

Jackson started looking around, apparently searching for cameras. "Let's hope."

Just as we reached his car, six police cruisers converged on the area, their headlights nearly blinding us. We raised our hands high in the air before they could even tell us to do so.

"What happened here?" one of the officers yelled, as he nervously approached us with his gun drawn.

"Which one of you blew this guy's brains out?" asked another cop, his voice overly animated as he stared down at what was left of Prentice.

"Jesus Christ!" the first officer gasped as he eyed Prentice's body.

"You're under arrest," he said, turning back to us. "Both of you."

Chapter 41

JACKSON

Mackenzie and I, now wrapped in police-issued blankets, were both shackled to a wobbly table inside a dingy interrogation room at Inglewood police headquarters.

Two world-weary homicide detectives, one bespectacled and scraggly, the other bald, loomed over us doing a crappy rendition of the good cop, bad cop routine.

"That's really what happened," Mackenzie said to them. "We're telling you the truth."

"Use your brains," I added. "Why else would we both be sitting here in our goddamned pajamas?"

The bald detective leaned in. "How should we know? That's what we're waiting for you assholes to tell us."

"We told you," Mackenzie said. "You're just not listening."

The scraggly detective nudged his partner aside and said to us, "I am listening. Hey, I'm on your side. But we both know your story's just that—a story. Well-rehearsed, even, but still a story. At least admit that."

The bald detective grabbed my blanket and yanked me close enough to smell coffee on his breath. "You think this is a joke, smart-ass? Or should I call you a rat? I knew your former partner." He drew back a fat fist. "I should punch your clock just for that shit alone."

Glancing up at the security camera mounted overhead, I said, "Either that thing is broken or you're ready for a career change— asshole."

Baldy's eyes narrowed and his jaw tightened, but, just as I expected, his fist never moved. Scraggly grabbed Baldy's arm. "Settle down. Just let me handle this."

"We'd like to call a lawyer," I said.

Scraggly snorted. "Oh, you wanna lawyer up? No problem. But not tonight. We're going to process your asses and you two will be sleeping in the shittiest cell we got."

I was ready to explode. "If you think—"

The door flew open and Lieutenant Gooden strode into the room.

Scraggly and Baldy were just as surprised as we were by the dapper detective's sudden appearance.

Lieutenant Gooden shook his head at us like a disappointed dad. "Didn't I tell you two to be careful? And what's with the blankets?"

"Whoa, buddy," Baldy said to Lieutenant Gooden. "Who the hell are you?"

"Yeah," Scraggly said. "And what the hell are you doing in my interrogation room?"

Lieutenant Gooden poked the ID card dangling around his neck. "LAPD. Lieutenant Mark Gooden, head of the organized crime unit. You two want to catch me up?"

"Catch you up?" Scraggly said. "This happened in Inglewood, not LA. This is our collar."

"Here's the way it works," Lieutenant Gooden said. "Anyone on OCU's watch list gets killed, like Big Ced's son, it automatically hits my desk. And no, I'm not pulling your case. I'm pulling my case. You two got a problem with that, take it up with your lieutenant."

Scraggly and Baldy both lowered their heads. They obviously didn't see a lot of action.

"So," Lieutenant Gooden said, "what have they told you so far?"

Scraggly chuckled. "They claim that Prentice Willis burglarized Ms. Cunningham's home. They chased him in Mr. Jones's car. A fight broke out and they killed Willis in self-defense."

"Come, on," Baldy said to Lieutenant Gooden, "Prentice Willis a burglar? Is that not the most ridiculous shit you ever heard?"

Lieutenant Gooden turned to us, his face unreadable. "Well," he said. "Is that really your story?"

"More or less," I said. "Yeah, that's how it went down."

He shifted his focus solely to Mackenzie. "You are backing him up on this?"

"Yep. Prentice tried to kill us," Mackenzie said. "It was him or us."

"You see," Scraggly said. "Total bullshit."

"I know these two and I believe them," Lieutenant Gooden said. "They're free to go. Cut 'em loose."

Mackenzie and I sat up as if we had both received an electric shock.

Did he just say we could go?

Scraggly and Baldy were gaping and doing double takes. "I'm sorry," Scraggly said. "We can't just let them go. They killed a guy."

Lieutenant Gooden pinned the two befuddled cops with stern eyes. "My case. Not yours. If Mr. Jones and Ms. Cunningham are not out of this building in ten minutes, I'm not calling your lieutenant. I'm waking up your captain. Just do it."

Then Lieutenant Gooden turned to us. "Don't leave town until this mess is all sorted out. Good night."

Mackenzie and I thanked Lieutenant Gooden and waved good-bye as he marched out.

Scraggly and Baldy just stared at us, mouths agape, dazed and confused.

I understood completely. I had no idea what had just happened, and I didn't want to wait around long enough for someone to figure it out and change their mind. I rattled my shackles and said to them, "Sorry to interrupt your drooling session, boys, but my partner and I are kinda in a rush."

Chapter 42

MACKENZIE

Something doesn't feel right," I said, as we waited outside the police station for the Uber that Jackson had just ordered. The only thing on our minds right now was returning to the scene of the crime to retrieve that lockbox, along with Jackson's Benz.

"You're right," Jackson said. "I don't understand why your boyfriend let us go."

"He's not my boyfriend."

"Did you sleep with him?" Jackson asked. "Is that why he let us go? You can tell me. You two are both consenting adults. It's no big deal."

I smiled.

"I knew it!" Jackson said, nearly jumping up and down. "You have absolutely no taste in men."

All I could do was laugh. "I did not sleep with the lieutenant. So please don't ask me again."

He stared at me as if he were trying to find the true answer in my face. "Not buying it. Why else would he let us go, except to save you, Macky."

I quietly gritted my teeth and decided not to ask him, yet again, to refrain from calling me that. If I did, he'd only intensify his taunts just to annoy me.

I winked at him. "A girl never tells."

"See, I knew it. You—"

I walked away as our Uber—a sleek silver Jaguar—pulled up.

"Nice ride," Jackson said, admiring the car. "Uber Black, of course."

"If I owned a Jaguar and had to drive Uber to pay for it," I said as the car rolled to a stop in front of us, "I'd buy a cheaper car."

Jackson sucked his teeth. "Maybe the guy is super rich and just likes driving. For all you know, he could suffer from nighttime anxiety and this is how he calms himself down."

"Whatever," I said, climbing into the back seat.

Our driver was a thin white kid who barely looked old enough to drive. We gave him our Uber code and were on the way back to the park.

"Nice ride," Jackson said to the guy, touching the soft leather of the back seat with jealous admiration.

"Thanks," the kid said. "It's my dad's."

Jackson gave me a satisfied glare, then sent me a text.

See. Told you he was rich.

I texted him back.

No he's not. His dad may be rich, but he isn't. He can't even afford his own car.

You're a snob.

Wow, I guess the pot is calling the kettle black.

Jackson texted me again, but I turned my phone face down on my lap and stared out of the window.

We were in a world of trouble. Prentice was dead and we were responsible for his death. Yet we'd walked out of the police station like we'd just been involved in a fender bender. It didn't make sense. But right now, Big Ced, not the cops, was my biggest concern. Would the crime don care that we were acting in self-defense? Even though Prentice was trying to take down his father and orchestrated all of this drama, he was still Big Ced's only son. Would he want to kill us for taking his blood or praise us for thwarting Prentice's power grab? I wanted to talk to Jackson about what we should do after retrieving the lockbox, but we couldn't talk in front of the driver and I didn't feel like texting.

So I spent the rest of the ride silently plotting our next move. Option one: We'd arrange a meeting with Big Ced to turn over the evidence, but refuse to show up until we received assurances that no one would harm us. That was a stupid idea. Even if Big Ced made us that promise, there was nothing to keep him from putting a bullet in our heads the second we turned over the lockbox.

Option two: Maybe we'd forgo a face-to-face meeting and just have the box messengered to Big Ced, then do a disappearing act like Jackson had suggested. That wasn't a great idea either. I had no desire to live my life on the run, and who's to say they wouldn't find us anyway.

I rested my head against the window, closed my eyes, and tried to come up with another, more workable option.

Jackson must've been lost in similar thought because he didn't text me or even speak for the rest of the ride. When we finally reached the park, Jackson yelped when he spotted his Benz.

"Look at my baby," he whimpered.

"It's not that bad," I said.

And all things considered, it wasn't. The Benz was pretty scratched up, but otherwise appeared drivable.

"Hang on for a minute," I said to the driver. "We need to make sure our car starts before you leave."

As Jackson ran over to his Mercedes, I headed for the trash bin where we'd hidden the lockbox, which was only a few yards away. Before I got there, I heard the pleasant sound of the revving of Jackson's engine.

He opened the car door and yelled out to the driver. "We're good," he said. "You can leave."

As the driver pulled off, Jackson jogged over to me.

"Why are you just standing there? Get the box."

I couldn't speak. Or even breathe.

"What's wrong with you?"

My words were halting. "It's . . . not . . . here."

Jackson moved me aside and reached his arm behind the trash bin. But he couldn't find it either.

"It's gone," I said, starting to panic.

Jackson wasn't hearing it. "It's only been a couple of hours. There's no way anyone saw us place it there. The way you shoved it back there, it's probably just stuck."

I watched as Jackson tried again, struggling to stretch his arm even farther behind the bin. When he came up empty, he stepped back and pushed the bin away from the wall, grunting as he used every ounce of his strength.

Once he'd pulled the huge bin several feet away from the wall, we both just stood there, staring.

The lockbox was gone.

Chapter 43

JACKSON

The sight of that empty space behind the trash bin seemed to open a pit in my gut—a radiating hollowness that weakened my knees.

Mackenzie, also gaping at the spot where the box used to be, grabbed my arm and squeezed. "So now what are we going to do?"

"I don't know," I said. "But I think I'm going to be sick."

Exactly two hours and eight minutes had transpired between Mac and me stashing our treasure and returning to find it gone. Even in that relatively small span of time absolutely anyone could've dug it up and taken the box—anywhere.

"How could this happen?" Mackenzie said. "Who the hell goes around searching behind trash bins in the middle of the night?"

I froze, Mackenzie's question striking me like a hard slap. Sense suddenly knocked back into me.

"No one goes searching behind trash bins in the middle of the night," I said, "unless they saw you hide something first."

Mackenzie's eyes widened. "You think someone saw us hide the box."

"Nothing else makes sense."

"Shhhh." I raised my palm in the air. "You hear that?"

"It's faint," Mackenzie finally said, "but I do hear something. Tapping. No, banging. Like someone's banging on something."

"I'll bet you a gazillion dollars," I said, "that sound is someone trying to open our box."

Without another word, Mackenzie and I dashed across the dark expanse of patchy grass; with each stride the metallic tapping sound grew louder and louder. We hit the brakes at the edge of a dirt footpath. On the opposite side, nestled amid a stand of overgrown bushes, stood a large blue-and-orange tent. A rusted shopping cart, overloaded with junk, was parked with care beside the tent, much like a family car outside a suburban home.

That constant banging, now unmistakably the sound of metal pounding metal, emanated from inside the tent—along with the warm glow of light.

I pulled back a piece of the tarp covering the tent and saw an elderly Black man sitting on the ground, hammer in hand, our box placed between his spindly legs. His bushy white beard and matching dreadlocks made me wonder for an instant if Santa had been evicted from the South Pole.

"Hey! You trespassin' on me private property!" he yelled in a thick Jamaican accent.

"We just want our box back," Mackenzie said before I could get the words out.

The old Jamaican's chin jutted forward. "You threw it away. Finders keepers." He protectively wrapped his arms around the box.

"We didn't throw it away," Mackenzie said. "We were trying to hide it."

"Give me a hundred dollars," the man said. "I give yuh da box."

I wasn't in the mood for bartering with this guy. As I took a step forward, he raised the hammer threateningly, stopping me cold.

"No need for violence," Mackenzie said. "We don't mind giving you a reward, but we don't even have pockets right now."

The homeless Jamaican waved off the dilemma with an ashy hand. "Dis no problem." Then, grabbing a cell phone, he said, "CashApp, PayPal, Venmo, or Zelle. Which do yuh prefer?"

Chapter 44

MACKENZIE

Despite our severe sleep deprivation, Jackson and I stayed up the rest of the night, our eyes glued to the lockbox. We were determined that as long as it was in our possession, the lockbox would be under constant surveillance.

We'd woken up Nadine a couple of hours ago and instructed her to contact Willis Worldwide to set up a meeting with Big Ced and his cronies. It was now almost eight the next morning and we still hadn't heard back.

I was on my second can of Celsius, the energy drink doing little to jolt me from my drowsy state. The can I'd given Jackson sat unopened on the coffee table separating us. He'd told me he didn't need any artificial energy boosts, but I'd left it there anyway in case he changed his mind.

In contrast to my sluggishness, Jackson seemed full of tense energy. Right now, he was sitting as erect as a steel rod in an armchair across from me, but in a couple of minutes, he'd be pacing the length of my living room for the umpteenth time.

"I could make you some coffee," I said, though it was obvious his taut nerves didn't need any caffeine.

"Naw. I'm good. I'm operating on pure adrenaline. Why don't you go ahead and get some sleep? I'll watch the box."

"I'm way too hyped to sleep. I just want this all behind us."

"I'm with you on that," Jackson said.

"We should probably have something to eat. Want me to cook?" I asked, though I wasn't hungry and didn't have the energy or the desire to cook.

"No appetite," Jackson said.

I got up, went into the kitchen, and returned with two protein bars. I handed one to Jackson. "I'm ordering you to eat."

Instead of opening the bar, he slid it into his pocket. "Maybe later."

As I tore mine open and took a bite, I asked Jackson a question. "What do you think Big Ced is thinking right now? I mean, we're responsible for his son's death."

Jackson took a long time to respond. "I don't know." His voice was uncharacteristically soft. "I'm sure he's well aware now that Prentice was trying to take him down."

"Even so," I said. "Prentice was his son. His blood."

"His blood who was trying to betray him," Jackson said.

"Sounds like you're of the opinion that he won't be concerned about exacting revenge on us for Prentice's death."

Jackson shrugged. "Honestly, Mac, I have no idea."

"Maybe we should open the box and make a copy of the evidence for our own safety."

He chuckled derisively. "And exactly how would that keep us safe? Having that evidence was supposed to keep Vincent Keane safe, but it didn't."

"But Keane didn't die at the hands of Big Ced," I pointed out.

"But we don't know if Prentice went after Keane on his own or at the direction of his father. Even with Prentice out of the way, we're not safe as long as we have this information."

I took a second to think about what he'd just said.

"Okay, then, let's call Mark. We don't have to tell him we have the lockbox. But maybe we can share a little more with him about what's going on. He could help protect us."

Jackson shook his head. "Not a good idea either. Letting him know how deep we're into this could backfire on us. Badly. I have a feeling we haven't seen the last of your tall, handsome boyfriend. I'm still suspicious about why he let us walk out of the police station the way he did."

Jackson was right. I guess we really didn't have any options.

"So we're just going to trust that once we hand over the lockbox they won't kill us?"

"Pretty much," Jackson said, then smiled. "Don't forget what I said."

"And what's that?"

"There's honor among thieves."

I huffed. "Again, with that. Do you really believe that?"

"Kinda."

"Well, I don't. The words *thieves* and *honor* don't even belong in the same sentence."

For the next several minutes, we continued our lockbox lookout in silence.

"I'm surprised that Nadine hasn't called us back yet," I said, interrupting the quiet. "Maybe we should give her a call."

Jackson shook his head. "Let's wait a little longer. She'll call."

And about thirty minutes later, she did.

As Jackson placed his cell phone to his ear, I watched his face, hoping to gauge whether what he was hearing was good or bad.

After only a few seconds, he gently set his phone on the coffee table. Then he clasped his hands, closed his eyes, and hung his head.

"You're scaring me," I said. "What did Nadine say? Did they agree to a meeting?"

Jackson nodded.

"Where? And why do you look so worried?"

Again, he took his time responding. "I look worried because of where they want us to meet."

I knew Jackson was as nervous as I was, but I didn't appreciate the way he was parceling out information.

"Stop being so mysterious. Where do they want to meet us?"

"Outside Victorville."

"Okay," I said. "Where outside Victorville? An office building? A parking lot? Where?"

Jackson shook his head. "Nope."

"Can you please just tell me?" I said, unable to hide my annoyance.

"They want to meet us off highway eighteen, at an abandoned airplane hangar."

It took a few seconds for his words to register. "That's in the middle of nowhere."

Jackson's lips angled into a glum smile. "Exactly."

Chapter 45

JACKSON

We cruised northeast along Interstate 15 beneath a cloudless midday sky. Traffic conditions were LA normal, meaning too heavy to drive at the speed limit. We averaged fifty miles an hour, which wasn't terrible. We'd make better time once we cleared the metro area.

Usually, whenever I found myself coaxing my Mercedes along I-15, my destination would almost always be Las Vegas. Just me, flying solo, headed for a few carefree nights of drinking, gambling, and if I got really lucky, hooking up with some lovely stranger also looking to burn off some steam.

But today was different. Today, I was not alone. I had Mackenzie riding shotgun beside me, and a two-foot-square metal box of trouble resting on the back seat. And instead of a fun time in Sin City, Mac and I were on our way to a virtual gangster convention in the middle of bum-fuck nowhere. So, in a manner of speaking, you could still say that we were going to Sin City—but not for fun.

During the long drive Mackenzie and I barely spoke. While unusual for us, the lack of conversation felt right for this particular journey. Besides, there wasn't much to say. We both knew what we had to do, and that was that. Talking about it would just make us more nervous—if that was possible. So, instead, we tried to soothe ourselves with good music and watched the world slide by.

After about twenty-five minutes, traffic thinned, and we were doing a steady seventy-five. Still traveling along the 15, LA's skyline and its surrounding suburbs finally disappeared behind the sparse rolling foothills of the San Gabriel Mountains. Leaving the big city behind, along with any sense of security a heavily policed area provides, had me gripping my steering wheel a little tighter.

I noticed Mackenzie, more and more, shifting uncomfortably in her seat. No doubt, like me, she was unnerved by the increasingly isolated and unfamiliar landscape that stretched out before us.

Just south of Victorville, we exited I-15 onto Route 18 west, a relentlessly straight two-lane highway that sliced across the outskirts of the Mojave Desert. The landscape now surrounding us was an unyielding flat expanse of nothing but scrub brush and the occasional Joshua tree. The silhouette of mountains loomed in the distance beneath an ocean of stark blue sky. The barren high desert scenery, while beautiful, was also overwhelming, making me feel small and a little helpless. Anything could happen to anyone out here—and no one would know.

After traveling eight miles without passing anything man-made, not even a damn billboard, we left Route 18, turning right onto a dirt road called Sheep Creek Pass. Tires crunching and kicking dust, we sped north toward a mountainous horizon, across what was essentially open desert.

Mackenzie and I glanced at each other; no words needed. Our eyes said it all.

Are we really doing this?

The farther we sped away from civilization, the more unfriendly the road became. Before long, we were pretty much off-roading in a slightly dented, ninety-thousand-dollar luxury vehicle. Despite my AMG's Advanced Sport Suspension, we were getting a good jostling, as was the rattling metal box in the rear seat. I never had much love for Mackenzie's Jeep, but at that moment I dearly missed that old heap.

Then, just like that, the ride went eerily smooth. The dirt road now behind us, we zoomed across an immense, wide-open stretch of salt flats. The white-streaked, perfectly level terrain seemed unnatural, as if we were driving across an alien world.

Mackenzie and I exchanged looks again.

Okay, this is getting nuts.

According to the directions we'd received, the abandoned airfield should've been close, but I couldn't see a goddamn thing.

Mackenzie pointed straight ahead. "I think that's it over there."

As we continued forward, the elongated profile of an airplane hangar, once naturally camouflaged, began to stand out from the distant mountains behind it.

"There's nothing else out here," I said. "That's definitely it."

Drawing ever closer, we soon had a better view of the abandoned old hangar. The enormous wood-slatted building had a sagging, curved roof, countless broken windows, and had been sunbaked for at least half a century to the point of extra crispy.

Outside the hangar's huge open doors, a dozen or so parked vehicles glinted in the sun—a virtual auto show of luxury sedans, high-end SUVs, and exotic sports cars.

We could also see several figures standing sentry near the hangar's entrance. We couldn't make out faces yet, but there was no mistaking the ominous elongated profiles of the automatic weapons they each held.

And yet we kept going.

I shut off the radio and said to Mackenzie, "You ready?"

"No. Not even a little bit. Are you?"

"Absolutely not."

We shared a nervous chuckle, then I said to her, "Just remember, no matter how sideways things get, never let them see you sweat."

Mackenzie made a face. "I don't think that applies in the desert."

"Yeah, maybe you're right. We just need to hold our shit together."

"Agreed."

Suddenly the old hangar loomed large over us. We had arrived.

Under the watchful eyes of a trio of armed goons standing outside the hangar, I wheeled into a spot next to a black Lamborghini SUV with a vanity plate that read: BLKDTH.

As Mackenzie and I climbed out of my now-sand-blasted Mercedes, I couldn't help admiring that Lambo. Maybe instead of repairing my car, I'd lease a Lambo, I mused, if we got out of this alive and somehow received our payday.

Mackenzie and I started toward the hangar. The temperature was in the low 80s, not bad for the desert. The air was crisp and clean, despite a faint, dry, dusty scent.

After going just three steps we both froze in our tracks.

"I believe we forgot something." Mackenzie said.

"Ya think?"

I returned to my car and grabbed the metal box from the back seat, then Mac and I continued to the hangar door.

The three guards, one Black, one Caucasian, and one Mexican, each a representative of one of our underworld clients, greeted us by leveling their assault rifles.

"Hands up," ordered Big Ced's henchman.

"We're not armed," I said. "We left 'em in the car, like the instructions said."

He motioned sharply with his weapon. "I said hands up!"

Still gripping the box, I raised my hands overhead. Mackenzie did the same.

The Black guard kept his weapon trained on us, while the other two patted us down. The white guy did me, and the Mexican did Mackenzie. The two goons were thorough and surprisingly professional; I'll give them that. A reassuring glance from Mackenzie told me that the goon behaved himself.

Satisfied, my guard nodded to the gaping door behind him. "Go ahead. They're waiting for you."

After stepping from the bright, sunlit desert into the subdued interior of the old hangar, we paused to give our eyes a second to adjust.

The interior was cavernous. Slanted rays of sunlight sliced through damaged patches in the roof. Cobwebs clung to the rafters, so huge and perfect they resembled Halloween decorations. Machinery and airplane parts, unrecognizable beneath decades of rust, hugged the walls. Then there was the smell, a mélange of old wood, dirt, decay, and—grilling steak.

Directly ahead of us, at the very center of the hangar's interior, the criminals that Mackenzie and I had come to meet were enjoying a barbecue lunch.

With a dozen heavily armed men standing guard behind them, Big Ced, Mateo Meza, and Yaron Bioff lounged side by side at a cloth-draped banquet table, idly picking at salads and sipping red wine.

Nearby, a chubby thug wearing a grease-splattered apron and a shoulder-holstered gun manned a large charcoal grill, skillfully using tongs to flip thick slabs of meat. Smoke wafted up past the rafters, escaping the hangar through its tattered roof.

That brother certainly knew something about grilling, because those steaks smelled amazing.

Big Ced, a napkin draped over his blue pinstriped three-piece suit, spotted us lingering by the door. With a hearty wave, he beckoned us forward. "Don't just stand there," his voice boomed across the immense space. "Come. Come."

Our footsteps crunched on debris-strewn concrete as Mackenzie and I, the metal box firmly in my grasp, moved deeper into the vast building and sidled up to the table.

Unlike Big Ced, who was seated between them, Meza and Bioff didn't bother to dress for the occasion. Meza, dripping bling, sported another custom-embroidered hoodie, while Bioff, still rocking his signature pinkie ring, wore a beige Polo windbreaker over a white dress shirt.

For a fleeting instant, all three men couldn't resist eyeballing the metal box at my side, before greeting us with respectful nods.

There were only two other chairs at the table, both vacant and positioned directly opposite the three crime bosses. Fork in hand, Big Ced gestured to the chairs. "Sit, please. Have some lunch."

Man, the aroma of those sizzling steaks made my mouth water. But Mac and I weren't interested in socializing with these killers, we just wanted to wrap this shit up fast, then get back to living our lives. Emphasis on living.

A "hell no" glance from Mackenzie screamed that she was on the same page.

Putting on a respectful smile, I said to Big Ced, "That's very nice of you, sir, but if you don't mind, we'd like to just conclude our business as quickly as possible."

"Yes," Mackenzie added. "We'd rather just get this done so you three can finish enjoying your lunch. It looks good, by the way."

Big Ced's features darkened. As if Mackenzie and I had just ruined his appetite, he set down his fork hard, the sharp sound echoing through the hangar. "Can you believe this?" he said to Meza and Bioff. "These two killed my son, and now they insult me by rejecting my hospitality."

The other crime bosses shook their heads disapprovingly but kept stuffing their faces.

Big Ced peered up from the table at the two of us with ice-cold eyes. "How dare you disrespect me in front of my friends here?"

For what felt like an eternity, Mackenzie and I just stood there, frozen. Expressionless. I'd bet anything that if I could place my hand on her chest, I'd feel her heart pounding as fast as mine. Swallowing into a dry throat, I struggled to remain composed as I forced words out. "Mr. Willis, with all due respect, as you know, Prentice tried to kill us, not to mention his plans to take you all down so he could run things. In the end we had no choice. That said, we are truly sorry that—"

Big Ced raised a hand. "Excuse me. You're truly sorry for what exactly?"

Mackenzie and I blinked with confusion. Was this guy not listening or was he having a stroke?

"Mr. Willis," Mackenzie said, "Jackson and I are sorry for having killed your son."

"I see," Big Ced said with a pensive nod—and what came next was so unexpected that our reaction was impossible to conceal. "Here's the thing," he went on. "Prentice wasn't really my son."

"What?" Mackenzie and I gasped in unison.

"He was my stepson, and to be honest, I never completely trusted that ambitious son of a bitch. I should've known better than to let him take point on something so important. So, the way I see it, you two did me a favor by killing that bastard. Thank you."

With that Big Ced picked back up his fork and resumed eating his salad.

Mackenzie and I exchanged "what-the-fuck-just-happened" looks.

"So, wait," I said to Big Ced. "All that jazz before, you were just fucking with us?"

"None of that was serious?" Mackenzie asked. "Seriously?"

Big Ced chuckled. "Sorry, but I couldn't resist. Anyway, it was Mateo's idea."

Mateo Meza wagged his fork at us. "I gotta give you two props. You kept your cool. That took real cojones."

"He's right," Bioff said. "You two got chutzpah. I respect that. You two are something special."

"Thanks, I think," Mackenzie said. Then we both laughed, and it was a relief to let off a little tension. For the first time in minutes, Mackenzie and I both breathed normally.

There was a brief pause when the grill master finally served up the main course. As the crime bosses sliced into perfectly cooked medium-rare prime rib, Big Ced repeated his offer for Mackenzie and me to join them. Watching these apex predators shove bloody meat into their mouths was reason enough to respectfully reiterate our desire to get paid and get the hell out of there.

"All right," Big Ced said, gnawing on meat and gesturing to the metal box, "let's see what you got."

I placed the metal box on the table before the three men.

Big Ced pointed to the padlock. "I don't suppose you got a key for that?"

"We don't," Mackenzie said.

"Not a problem." Big Ced snapped his finger and one of the armed goons standing behind him stepped forward holding a large bolt cutter. "Open it," Big Ced ordered.

As the goon rounded the table with the bolt cutter, I raised a hand and said, "Hold on." The goon stopped in his tracks. Then, turning to Big Ced, I continued, "First we'd like to get paid—if you don't mind."

Big Ced stopped chewing and stared at me as he slowly wiped his mouth with a napkin. Finally, he said, "We don't even know what's in the box yet."

"Actually," Mackenzie said, "we know exactly what's in the box. Let's be real. What else could it be?"

"And if we're wrong," I added, gesturing to the army of goons behind him, "you can just take your money back."

Big Ced, with just a couple of glances, surveyed his two colleagues.

Meza and Bioff simply shrugged and kept eating.

Big Ced nodded. "Okay, let's get you paid." He snapped his fingers again and another armed goon rounded the table carrying a black briefcase.

Mackenzie took the case, laid it on the table, popped the latches, and swung it open.

It was all there. Fifteen fat packets of circulated one-hundred-dollar bills, each wrapped tight with a yellow $10,000 paper strap.

My palms began to sweat. The fact that they'd actually brought the cash boosted my confidence that Mac and I would walk out of there alive—and one hundred and fifty grand richer.

"You want to count it?" Big Ced asked.

"Nah," I said, "I believe we're good." I turned to my partner. "Right?"

"Absolutely," Mackenzie said, shutting the briefcase and removing it from the table.

I turned to the goon standing by with the bolt cutter and gestured to the metal box on the table. "Have at it." But the goon didn't budge until Big Ced gave him a nod.

Mackenzie and I watched the bolt cutter slice through the padlock with ease. The goon removed what was left of the lock and slid the metal box across the table, within reach of the three bosses.

Big Ced pushed his half-finished plate of steak aside and drew the box closer to him, as if it were another gourmet dish that he was about to enjoy.

Bioff and Meza set down their utensils and wiped their mouths, their full attention now on Keane's box as well.

With zero ceremony, Big Ced flipped open the box's lid and removed the three notebooks and the cover letter detailing Keane's instructions. After briefly showing the document to Mateo and Bioff, he handed each man the notebook bearing his name.

All three men skimmed through Keane's handwritten notes. Each expressionless, only pages turning and eyes moving. After about five minutes they were all done reading. Big Ced collected all three notebooks and the letter and waved over the grill master. Handing everything over to the burly man, Big Ced said, "Make these well done."

"Yes, sir," the grill master replied. Returning to the grill, he tossed the three notebooks and the letter onto the rack, doused them with lighter fluid, then used a grill lighter to set them ablaze.

WOOSH!

Everyone in that hangar, including Mackenzie and me, watched in silence as Keane's dangerous little notebooks burned so hot that the heat prickled my face. In moments, there was nothing left but the lingering scent of charred paper and a small pile of ashes.

Big Ced raised his wineglass to me and Mackenzie, and Meza and Bioff followed suit. "To a job well done," the crime boss said to us. "Bravo."

All three men downed their wine in one gulp.

"Okay, then," I said to the trio, putting on a closer's smile. "We're definitely happy that you're happy."

"Yes, nice doing business with you," Mackenzie lied. "It was definitely a unique experience."

"So, if there's nothing else," I said, both Mac and I beginning to back away, "we're gonna get out of here. Thank you."

"Thank you very very much," Mackenzie said, raising the briefcase.

Then we both turned to leave, but before we could take a single step, Big Ced's even voice ceased us. "Actually, there is one more thing."

I shifted my gaze from the hangar door before us, so close yet so far, to meet Mackenzie's nervous eyes. Both of us thinking the exact same thing.

Oh shit.

Big Ced's voice came again. "Just one tiny detail. Won't take a second."

Slowly, Mackenzie and I turned back around to face Big Ced, Mateo Meza, and Yaron Bioff.

I swallowed, forced a smile, and said, "Yeah, what's up?"

Then Meza began to laugh at us while Bioff shook his head woefully.

And that's when we knew. That's when my stomach flip-flopped, my breathing quickened, and my legs began to turn to noodles. That's when the briefcase began to tremble in Mackenzie's grip.

Big Ced signaled and three armed goons quickly approached us. One goon snatched the briefcase from Mackenzie and placed it back on the banquet table. The other two pressed the muzzles of their AR-15s to our skulls and forced us down on our knees.

Our plan not to let them see us sweat meant nothing when faced with certain death. The steel muzzle felt ice cold against my scalp. My entire body was a trembling bundle of tight cords, my thrumming heart smacking my rib cage. Mackenzie, panting, fist clenched tight, glared at Big Ced.

"Why?" she pushed out through gritted teeth. "Whyyyy?"

Then Big Ced's answer filled the hangar, like the voice of doom. "It's nothing personal. I have a strict no-loose-strings policy. Sorry— and goodbye." Then, with a casual nod of the head, Big Ced signaled our two executioners to blow our brains out.

Mackenzie and I locked eyes. No words. No tears. A silent goodbye. She really was the best partner a guy could ask for.

The click of the weapon's safety release startled us, shattering the moment.

She squeezed her eyes shut and I did the same.

Instead of a gunshot . . . I heard voices shouting, "Police! Drop your weapons! We have the hangar surrounded!"

Mackenzie and I opened our eyes to a scene of complete chaos. The two gunmen who had held us at gunpoint were now firing in all directions as dozens of SWAT agents, all garbed in desert camouflage, swarmed the hangar.

Some agents rushed in through the open door, others rappelled from the ceiling, still others breached the hangar's walls with precision explosives and charged in.

While Big Ced, Meza, and Bioff hid behind the overturned banquet table, their armed goons bravely exchanged automatic gunfire with the crack assault team.

Bullets zinging over our heads, I yelled to Mackenzie, "Come on!" Then, keeping our heads low, we ran, leaped over the grill master's dead body, and took cover behind the grill. As bullets dinged against our makeshift shield, Mackenzie pried a Glock from the grill master's limp hand.

"Hey," I said. "I want a gun too."

After checking the clip, Mackenzie began firing at the goons.

One goon was stupid enough to charge directly toward us. Mac dropped that sucker with a perfect shot. When he smacked the concrete, his AR-15 popped free and skittered to a stop right beside me.

"Happy?" Mackenzie said.

Damn skippy.

Still ducked behind the grill, Mackenzie and I blasted as many goons as we could, until our weapons clicked empty.

Not much longer after that the shoot-out was over.

The SWAT agents were busy rounding up and handcuffing the lucky ones.

Mackenzie and I emerged from our hiding spot in time to see the black briefcase filled with our money being tagged as evidence and sealed. What made up for this heartbreaking sight was the satisfying spectacle unfolding just a few feet away.

The three big shots—Big Ced, Mateo Meza, and Yaron Bioff—surrounded by agents, were each being handcuffed and shackled like common criminals.

Big Ced spotted us, but said nothing, just fixed us with a murderous glare.

I said to Mackenzie, "I'm pretty sure our former client thinks we set him up."

"Did we?" Mackenzie said, scratching her head. "I mean—what the hell happened here?"

"Yeah—good question."

The answer came from a familiar voice behind us. "I'm really glad to see that you two are okay."

It was Lieutenant Gooden, also garbed in desert camo, striding toward us with a big smile. I had to give it to him, the bastard looked even better in assault gear.

"Mark," Mackenzie said. "You're responsible for this?"

"In a way," he said. "My task force, in coordination with the state police and SWAT, but yeah, this is pretty much my show."

"Show?" Mackenzie asked. "What are you talking about?"

"In other words," I said to the lieutenant, "thanks for saving our lives—now what the hell is going on?"

Before Gooden could answer, Big Ced, who was now being led away, barked, "Gooden! You're too late. The evidence is gone, and Keane is dead. You got nothing!"

Lieutenant Gooden signaled the officers escorting Big Ced to hold up, then he squared off with the handcuffed crime boss. "That's where you're wrong, Willis. Vincent Keane is very much alive, safe in protective custody. As for those three notebooks, the ones you burned were copies. The originals are in an LAPD safe. But really, we don't need the originals—I have digital copies."

Gooden pulled out his iPhone and held it up to Big Ced's widening eyes. "Would you like to see?"

"That's a fucking lie!" Big Ced shouted. "You're lying!"

Lieutenant Gooden flicked his hand and the escorting officers muscled a furious Big Ced away.

Meanwhile Mackenzie and I were having a full-on gaping contest. I was tempted to look around the hangar for hidden cameras because an elaborate prank would actually make more sense.

Mackenzie grabbed Lieutenant Gooden's arm and spun him around to face her. "Was it a lie, Mark? That stuff about Keane being alive and the notebooks being fake. Was it a lie or not?"

Lieutenant Gooden sighed and laid a hand on Mackenzie's shoulder. "Look, Macky, there's a lot going on. No time to explain now. Let's talk about this back at the station, okay?"

Then Gooden simply walked away.

Mackenzie blinked, then turned to me. "I can't believe him."

"Forget that asshole. Told you he was no good for you. We need to be glad we're still breathing."

Mac's shoulders slumped as the truthfulness of my words seemed to register.

"C'mon, partner." I threw an arm around her and we started trudging toward my car. "Let's go have a stiff drink."

Mac stopped walking and turned to look at me. "No way. We're going straight to LAPD Headquarters. Mark played us. Or more correctly, he played me. And I plan to find out why."

Chapter 46

MACKENZIE

By the time we made it to police headquarters two hours later, I was still as hot as a skillet. Jackson and I had been sitting alone in an interrogation room for the past forty-five minutes waiting for answers. The longer we waited, the angrier I got.

I was particularly perturbed that Jackson wasn't even half as upset as I was.

He pulled out the protein bar I'd given him earlier and ripped it open. "Want some?" he asked.

"No," I snapped. "Why are you so damn happy? Aren't you pissed about what just went down? Lieutenant Gooden used us."

"In situations like this," Jackson said, talking and chewing at the same time, "I'm just glad to be alive."

At that moment, Lieutenant Gooden lumbered into the room, smiling like he'd just won the lottery.

"How are my two favorite private investigators?"

"We're pretty pissed off," I said, jumping to my feet.

"Awww, don't be mad," the lieutenant said. He pulled out a chair and sat down across from us.

"What the hell is this all about?" I demanded.

"Have a seat," he said, propping his right ankle upon the opposite knee, "and I'll tell you."

I slowly sat back down, locking my arms across my chest.

"Let me apologize for my partner's demeanor," Jackson said. "She can be a real hothead at times."

"You don't need to apologize for me," I said to Jackson, but never taking my eyes off Lieutenant Gooden. "I can speak for myself. You used us."

"Used you?" The lieutenant paused and scratched his forehead. "I wouldn't call it using you. At least not in the technical sense. You two were all wrapped up in this from the start. It's not like you were entrapped or something."

"Is Keane really alive?" Jackson asked.

"Sure is," Gooden said. "Alive and safe and sound in protective custody."

"And you have copies of all the evidence he compiled on the crime bosses?" Jackson continued.

"Every last bit of it."

"But how did you get it?" he asked.

"Once Keane came out of his coma, he was scared shitless. He figured the guy who tried to kill him was sent by one of the crime bosses and that he would likely return to finish the job. So he called me up and begged to be put into protective custody. Told us about the burial plot and what it contained, so of course we dug it right up."

My mind fogged by anger, I shook my head. "I don't get it. Once you had the incriminating evidence, why put Jackson and me in danger?"

"I knew you two were mixed up with those three criminals," Lieutenant Gooden said, "but I didn't know exactly how. But once Keane told us about the dossiers he had put together, it wasn't much of a leap to assume that Big Ced and his cronies had hired you two to recover that information. I also assumed that when it came time for you two to deliver, Willis, Bioff, and Meza would once again gather in one spot, making it easy to bust them all. When I stopped by your office that day and made that comment about Keane taking his secret to the grave, I was counting on you two picking up on that. And you did. After that, me and my team just sat back and watched it all play out."

"So you lied," I said. "You were playing me all along."

"Awww, sorry about that, my sweetness. It's not like you didn't look me in the eye and tell me a few lies of your own. I was just working my case like you two were working yours."

"But my lies didn't put your life in danger," I shouted at him. "You let us go out to that hangar when you knew they'd kill us?"

"Stop being so melodramatic." The lieutenant casually angled his head. "I wasn't going to let that happen. You're alive, aren't you?"

"With all due respect," Jackson said, his tone no longer jovial, "you put us in a very dangerous position. We were seconds from death."

The lieutenant held up both palms. "Hey, you guys chose to get involved with those thugs. Danger like that comes with the territory. Don't try to blame me for your poor choices."

"You're an asshole," I said.

"Awww, my sweetness, sorry you feel that way. I was planning on inviting you out to dinner again so we could get to know each other a little better. I bet you're a little firecracker in bed."

"Too bad you'll never find out."

He laughed. "See, if you had played nice, I was going to let you keep that money. Now, I'm not."

With that, the lieutenant stood up. "A couple of my detectives need to interview you," he said. "So I need you to hang around a bit longer. And no more games. You need to come clean about every-thing you know."

Once he'd left the room, Jackson glared at me.

"You should've been nice to the guy. You just cost us six figures."

"Shut up. There was no way he was going to let us keep that money. And you know it."

"Maybe," Jackson said. "Well, at least there's one thing I know for sure."

He waited for me to inquire, but I refused to do so.

"I guess it wasn't true love for you and Lieutenant Goody after all. He definitely punked you."

I reared back and punched Jackson in the shoulder. Hard.

"Owww," he yelled, grabbing his arm, his twisted face exagger-ating his pain. "What was that for?"

"That was actually for the lieutenant. But since he's no longer in the room, you're the next best thing."

Chapter 47

JACKSON

What's that big papery thing you're reading?" I asked Mackenzie.

"Are you blind?" she said. "It's a newspaper."

"Whoa, they still make those? Or did you swipe it from a museum?"

"Don't you have anything better to do?"

"I wish I did."

"Yeah," she said with a sigh. "Me too."

It was a little after 10 a.m. on a Tuesday. Mackenzie and I were seated at our desks, essentially waiting for the phone to ring. A month had passed since Lieutenant Good-for-nothing used us as the cheese in his elaborate rat trap. In the weeks following we picked up a few quick gigs, here and there, mostly divorce-related, but nothing long-term and long on the green. Still, we weren't sweating it.

The fifty-grand advance we received from Big Ced was more than enough to give our fledgling agency a decent runway. Even after dropping a chunk of it on our new office decor, we still had enough to float the business for six months or so. In the end Mackenzie's reasoning won out and we settled on the best IKEA had to offer. Good thing, too, because I would've spent about three times more, and this little dry spell might've put Safe and Sound Investigations out of business. Of course, things would've been a whole lot different if we could've kept that briefcase stuffed with cash. I'll never know for sure if Mackenzie's attitude really soured Gooden on letting us keep that money. And I'll never stop wondering about it either.

"Okay," I said to Mackenzie, "I gotta ask. Why are you reading the *LA Times*?"

"I saw it in 7-Eleven," Mackenzie said, "and I couldn't resist. Look." She turned the paper to show me its cover.

Over a triptych photo of our former criminal clients the headline read: *An Empire Falls. DA Scores Historic Joint Indictment Against Cedric Willis, Yaron Bioff, and Mateo Meza.*

"Yeah," I said, "that's everywhere online. My favorite part is how the judge denied bail. Anyway, I still don't understand the newspaper."

Mackenzie shrugged. "I don't know. I'm gonna save it. Stick it in a scrapbook or something."

I laughed. "Scrapbooking? Nice. And when do you start collecting stray cats?"

Mackenzie put down the newspaper. "You know, I think you actually enjoy getting on my nerves. You got a problem with me, Mr. Jones?"

"Other than you costing us one hundred and fifty grand? Nah, we're good."

Mackenzie sighed. "I told you a thousand times, you big dummy, Mark just said that to piss us off. There's no way we could keep that money. I'm surprised the police didn't come after the fifty thousand advance."

"Hey, careful," I said. "Don't ever say that out loud again. I'm serious. Your ex-boyfriend could be listening."

Before Mackenzie's guaranteed Pavlovian response to my calling Gooden her boyfriend, we were interrupted by two quick knocks followed by my cousin pushing through the office door.

"Excuse me," Nadine said. "There's—"

"Actually," I said, cutting her off, "you're not excused."

"Pardon me?"

"What's the point of knocking if you're just going to barge in?" I turned to Mackenzie. "Back me up here."

Mackenzie sighed and said to Nadine, "I do see his point, but it's not a big deal."

"What do you mean *not a big deal*? It's unprofessional." I turned back to Nadine. "Go out, close the door, and try again."

Nadine laughed. "Look. I hear you, cuz, but if you're going to treat me like a damn five-year-old, I'll just go get me a job at McDonald's. They pay twenty dollars an hour to start now. Two dollars more than I make here, by the way."

"Look," I said, "I was kidding about doing it over, but let's keep it professional. Cool?"

"Sure," Nadine said. "And the pay should be professional too. I should at least earn more than a burger flipper." Mimicking me, she turned to Mackenzie. "Back me up here."

Mackenzie chuckled and said, "She does have a point. I think we should give her a raise. Let's make it twenty-one dollars an hour."

"What?" I said to my business partner. "You do realize we're slow right now, right?"

Mackenzie waved it off. "Sure, but things will pick up. Anyway, it's just a few dollars."

"Yeah, cuz," Nadine said. "It's just a few dollars. Come on."

I frowned at her. "Calling me *cuz* is not professional either."

"I meant Mr. Jones," Nadine said, grinning. "Pleeeeease."

"All right," I said, giving in. "Fine."

"Congratulations, girl," Mackenzie said, giving my cousin a wink.

Nadine pumped her fist. "Yes!" Then she rushed over and high-fived Mackenzie. SLAP!

"If you two are done being *professional*," I said, "can we get back to business?" Then to Nadine, "Why'd you come in here in the first place?"

"Oh yeah," she said. "Almost forgot. You have a walk-in waiting to see you. And get this, he has two big-ass bodyguards with him."

Trading looks, Mackenzie and I both shot up in our seats. "What's the man's name?" Mackenzie asked.

"It's the white dude who was in the coma," Nadine said. "You know—Vincent Keane."

"What?" I said to Nadine, pointing at the office door. "Are you telling me that Vincent Keane is out there right now?"

"Yeah," she said. "Like I told you, him and two huge bodyguards."

I groaned and shook my head. "Why didn't you tell us that from the start?"

"Because you interrupted me with all that knocking business."

Mackenzie raised a hand to me. "Jackson, shush." Then she turned to Nadine. "Could you please send Mr. Keane in? The bodyguards can wait out there."

Seconds later, Mr. Vincent Keane, adorned in a custom blue suit and supported by a single aluminum crutch, limped into our office. Compared to the photos provided to us by Prentice, Keane looked older and frailer now, clearly the toll of his awful accident and spending several days in a coma. Still, I recognized that long white hair, and when Keane smiled at us, like in the photos, his eyes still twinkled.

"Good morning," he said, his voice strong and earnest. "I believe I owe you two a thank-you for saving my hide."

Mackenzie and I rounded our desks and shook Keane's hand.

We offered him a seat, but he declined, explaining he couldn't stay long.

"It's good to see you on your feet, sir," Mackenzie said to him.

"Yeah," I added. "The last time we saw you, to be honest, you weren't looking too hot."

Keane laughed. "I bet. Well, as you can see, I look a little better now—thanks to you two. Lieutenant Gooden told me all about how you two fought off that hit man in my ICU room. And for that, Vincent Francisco Keane is now forever in your debt."

I'd never heard anyone, in real life, refer to themselves in the third person, but Keane somehow pulled it off.

"That's very nice of you to say, sir," Mackenzie said. "You're welcome."

"I appreciate that," I said to Keane. "Hey, maybe you can repay us by coming to the rescue the next time we get jumped."

Keane laughed again, then said, "Actually, I believe I have something far better. Lieutenant Gooden, such a nice man, also told me about the tremendous amount of money you two lost when Willis, Bioff, and Matco were arrested." Then he reached into his inside pocket and pulled out a white envelope. "Hopefully this will make up for that financial loss."

I grabbed that envelope before the man finished talking. "Thank you," I said. "That is very generous of—"

Mackenzie snatched the envelope from me and tried to hand it back to Keane. "That's a very nice gesture, Mr. Keane. But we can't accept it."

Keane raised a hand, refusing to take the envelope back. "But I insist," he said. "What I offer you is nothing short of life-changing."

Those words, *life-changing*, made my entire body tingle. Before she could say something else stupid, I snatched the envelope from Mackenzie. "Of course we can accept it," I said to Keane, smiling so hard my face hurt. "I'm sure I can speak for my partner here when I say we greatly appreciate your generosity." Then I pinned Mackenzie with desperate, pleading eyes. "Right, Mac?"

Mackenzie put on a smile for our generous guest. "Yes. Of course. A gift wasn't necessary, but thank you."

"Excellent," Keane said. "This makes me very happy."

Only after Keane and his bodyguards were gone, and the office door locked, did I dig that envelope out. Gazing at it, I said, "Did you hear him, Mac? Life-changing. I'm almost afraid to open it."

Mackenzie was back behind her desk, shaking her head at me. "Look at you. You act like there's a billion dollars in that envelope. Keane's rich—but he ain't that rich."

"It's all relative," I told her. "Life-changing for us could be a few million. Keane's got that covered easy."

"You really think it's that much?"

"People like Keane, people who know money, don't just idly throw around terms like *life-changing*. He said it for a reason. Yup, I think we're looking at millions."

Mackenzie chuckled. "Right now, we're just looking at a wrinkled white envelope. Open the damn thing already."

"Okay. Just relax."

"I'm relaxed. Open it!"

"Okay, okay," I said. "Here goes nothing." I could feel the vein in my neck pulse as I ripped open the flap, reached in, and pulled out—a folded letter.

"That doesn't look like a life-changing check," Mackenzie said.

"Hold on." First, I double-checked the envelope to see if there was anything else inside. Nothing. Next, I unfolded the letter, hoping a check would fall out. Still nothing.

I blinked and the room seemed to tilt a little. "I-I don't understand."

"Read the letter, silly," Mackenzie said. "Maybe it's banking instructions, or a cryptocurrency password, who knows."

My pulse quickened again. "You're right."

The letter was typewritten and straight to the point. I read it aloud.

Dear Mr. Jones and Ms. Cunningham,

For the invaluable service of saving my life I grant you both unlimited legal services for as long as I am able to practice law.

Thank You.
Vincent F. Keane Esquire

All my excitement drained out of me, leaving me hollow and weak. I dragged myself over to my desk and slumped into my chair.

To Mackenzie's credit she didn't laugh at me. She simply shook her head and said, "Goddamned lawyers."

I read the letter again to myself, then slapped it down on my desk. "You know what?" I said to Mackenzie. "This actually isn't bad. I mean, in our business we're going to need a lot of legal help. This little letter here is going to save us a lot of money. Is it life-changing? No. But it ain't half bad."

With that I stuck Keane's letter in my desk drawer, then I reclined and put my feet up. "Nope, it ain't half bad at all."

All this time Mackenzie never took her eyes off me. Finally, she said, "So let me get this straight. You're okay that there was no multi-million-dollar check in that envelope? You're good?"

"No, I'm completely and utterly devastated to the point of wanting to cry. In fact, it's taking me everything I have not to break down into a wailing, sobbing fit. And it would really help if we talked about something else now."

"Okay," Mackenzie said. "Just checking."

Thankfully there was a knock at the office door.

Mackenzie and I waited for Nadine to burst in as usual, but all we got was another two sharp knocks.

Mackenzie and I looked equally impressed. She gestured for me to have the honor.

"Come in," I called.

Nadine popped in and said, "We got another walk-in. He says his wife went missing for a week and now that she's home he wants to know where she's been."

"Interesting," Mackenzie said, sitting up in her seat. "Could be something there."

"How's he look?" I asked Nadine. "You know what I mean."

"Well, he's dressed really nice," she said. "And he's wearing a big fat Rolex."

"Really?" I said. "A fat Rolex is good. Anything else?"

"Oh yeah," Nadine said. "I left out the best part. He says his wife seems different now. Like she might be an impostor. Crazy, right?"

Mackenzie's eyebrows went up. "Now, that's different."

"So, what do you guys think?" Nadine asked. "Should I send him in?"

"Are you kidding?" I said, sitting up and buttoning my sports jacket. "Sounds like a damn good mystery."

Acknowledgments

To Sean deLone, our editor at Atria Books—thank you for your invaluable insight and unwavering enthusiasm for this book.

And a big thank-you to the rest of our Atria team—specifically Peter Borland, Libby McGuire, Holly Rice, Zakiya Jamal, Lacee Burr, and Paige Lytle. We truly appreciate all your hard work behind the scenes that made this book a reality.

And to our agent, Lucy Carson—your passion for *Sounds Like Trouble*, the second book in this series, matched your excitement for our first book, *Sounds Like a Plan*. As always, we appreciate your guidance and unwavering support.

AVAILABLE IN PAPERBACK AND EBOOK NOW

The first Jackson Jones & Mackenzie Cunningham thriller

Two rival private investigators – with an undeniable attraction – must work together to solve a missing person case.

'Exactly what do you think you're doing?'

Jackson Jones and Mackenzie Cunningham are both proud, hard-working private investigators with their own firms in Los Angeles. They've never met . . . until now.

Running into each other on the job, they're shocked to discover that they've both been hired to investigate the same missing person case. With professional tensions rising, there's also the complication of an undeniable attraction. As the very real possibility emerges that they've been set up to take the fall for a murder, they have no choice but to work together.

'Fresh and pacy and a lot of fun.' *CrimeTimeFM*